Love Beyond the HORIZON

Love Beyond the HORIZON

MADHU VAJPAYEE

Srishti
PUBLISHERS & DISTRIBUTORS

Srishti Publishers & Distributors
A unit of AJR Publishing LLP
212A, Peacock Lane
Shahpur Jat, New Delhi – 110 049
editorial@srishtipublishers.com

First published by
Srishti Publishers & Distributors in 2021

10 9 8 7 6 5 4 3 2 1

Printed and bound in India

"Beyond the horizon, the sky is so blue,
I have got more than a lifetime to live to love you!"

Bob Dylan

For my mom,
Mrs Ratna Tewary
(1944–2020)

Acknowledgement

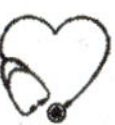

This book was made possible by the encouragement and support of my family and friends. There are so many of them to name here, but I am sure you know who you are and how much support you have given me in my writing journey.

As always, special thanks to Rasik, Mihika and Shubhankar Vajpayee for always being there for me and unconditionally supporting my writing work.

Thank you Manisha Sharma, for your optimism and unwavering support, which helped me navigate dark days.

Thanks to Shalini Malviya for your kind words of encouragement and good wishes.

Thank you Aruna Naidu, for your faith in me.

I am grateful to Srishti Publishers and the entire team for their support in bringing this book to life. Thank you Stuti, for reading and editing the manuscript and for your invaluable suggestions and feedback. Thank you Arup Bose, for always being there and taking a keen interest in every stage of the publishing process.

This book would not have been possible without all your help.

1

With the onset of winter, the fog had the entire city engulfed in its arms. The slight chill in the air made dusk more picturesque. School children returning home with their mothers in tow, youngsters roaming with friends, working executives rushing towards the warmth of their homes, all added to the busy evening in the beautiful city of Delhi.

In one corner of the road, a young man got out of the car and briskly walked towards the main building of Delhi Medical School and Hospital. Dressed in beige trousers with a blue shirt, he seemed to be in a hurry. For Dr Aakash Mehta, it was one of those long days at the hospital when there was an endless stream of patients arriving at the emergency department. Delhi was one of the worst hit by the flu pandemic. The list of patients seemed to swell up every hour. As a senior registrar, he not only had to see the patients, but also supervise the working of the unit.

It was already 6 p.m., but he hadn't had his lunch yet. Neither was it the first time he was facing something like this, nor was it going to be the last time. But somehow, he felt tired. Perhaps even more so as he hadn't slept well the previous night. He had rushed to the hospital to attend to an emergency patient. Routinely, two senior registrars were posted in the emergency department, but today he was managing everything alone. Dr Prakash Chandra had some urgent work at home, and the head of the medicine department, Dr Kapoor, was supposed to name a replacement. Still, there was no one in sight as of yet. It had been almost eighteen hours of non-stop work. He found himself feeling a little irritated.

Tossing his head, as though he would physically shake off something superfluous oppressing him, he proceeded to the next patient. He checked his face mask, adjusting it before beginning the examination of a ten-year-old boy with a high fever. He was coughing quite severely. One look at the patient and Dr Aakash knew that he was critical. He immediately ordered his admission and nasopharyngeal swab testing. He asked the nurse to give him the antiviral drug, Tamiflu.

As he turned to give instructions to his house officer, he caught a glimpse of her. She was walking towards him with small steps; looking lost in the commotion. There was something about her that caught his gaze. She was a tall, slim girl with an attractive face. Having never seen her on campus before, he wondered who she was. Before he could have thought anything else, she was standing before him.

"Dr Aakash Mehta?"

"Yes!" His face registered a look of surprise, soon replaced by the slow spread of the slight smile.

"I am Dr Avni Trivedi, junior registrar from Unit I. Dr Kapoor has asked me to do the emergency duty tonight." She introduced herself as briefly as possible as she caught the expression crossing his face.

He narrowed his eyes, "I see. So you are covering for Dr Prakash?"

"Yes." She looked up.

"Are you new to the hospital?" Aakash asked, unable to keep his curiosity to himself. "I have never seen you around before."

"I have just joined..." Her reply was like a whisper.

"I guess you are not from this medical school," he said, tilting his head.

When she didn't reply immediately, he raised his eyebrows seeking an answer from her.

She just shook her pretty head in denial. "I am from Allahabad Medical School." She did not give any more information than what was sought, and her face was expressionless. Aakash wondered if he was talking to a robot.

"So you have joined the post-graduation course here, in medicine… January batch," he said, thinking it'd be better to make assumptions rather than asking her. He didn't have the luxury to wait patiently for her answers. The Emergency ward was overflowing with patients and he needed to do her induction in the unit as soon as possible and get on with work.

Dr Kapoor had arranged for a junior registrar to cover for Dr Prakash. Dr Prakash would have been a great asset tonight, he thought, but he had to manage with the new person. He felt a rising surge of frustration again. Dr Kapoor should have considered the situation at hand, he felt. Trying to keep his feelings under control, he proceeded with the formalities.

"Welcome aboard, Dr Avni! Hope you enjoy your course here," he said as she handed over her documents to him. "But for now, you are in for a long haul!"

"Thanks! I will try my best," she said as their eyes met for the first time. For a brief second, he found himself looking for some change in her expression, but her face remained impassive. There was no sign of any excitement, or for that matter, any worry or jitters that one might feel in such a situation. Her aloofness had definitely succeeded in keeping her enigma intact, he thought. Soon, realizing that it was not the time to contemplate about her, he started introducing her to the department.

"It's a fifty-bedded facility. In all, we have six doctors on duty today. Besides us, there is one house officer, Dr Sanjay, and two interns, Dr Kamal and Dr Sandeep. Unfortunately, a few of our paramedical staff are also down with flu themselves, and as of now, there has been no replacement for them." Briefly, he again looked at her for any response. There was none. He continued, "You can see the rush. But don't get worked up. A lot of them are just here because of the fear; fear that it might be fatal. Fortunately, it's not as bad as it is made out to be."

She could see how he was trying to make her understand everything with hand gestures. The elegant lines of strain on the forehead and the dark circles around his eyes made him look tired, but they didn't overshadow his intelligent forehead and handsome face. She noticed, he was a tall man with an olive complexion and sharp features. His firm jawline was covered with a carefully trimmed beard. But it was his eyes that caught her attention the most. Intense yet dreamy, severe yet tender. His hair was a little shabby, with few strands out of place and falling haphazardly on his forehead. *Perks of being in such a busy profession*! She would have told him if she had met him a couple of years ago. The days when she made fun of every small thing that managed to catch her attention, when her life was like a breeze that felt so light, so fresh. The days when she was the unabridged Avni and not a robotic version of herself, which was bereft of any emotions, that could ever be tampered with.

"But no problem, we can survive." He smiled as he uttered those words. It was a deliberate smile to make her feel comfortable in the prevailing atmosphere. It was a part of his training. He had to learn how to treat a new employee; a young doctor at a new place, to be a good leader and a true professional. Armed with a gold medal in medicine, he was aspiring for a consultant job. He came from a family of doctors, his father being a paediatric surgeon and mother, a gynecologist. Fortunately, he had inherited the best genes from both of his parents. He was a brilliant doctor, very driven, to the point of being pedantic at times, a trait that often worked as an irritant for the hospital staff.

She just kept nodding her head in agreement, realizing that people like him leave no room for any error. She was reminded of a professor from her medical school who they had nicknamed Mr Perfectionist. But along with perfection, she could sense an air of subtle arrogance flickering through his eyes.

Aakash then gestured towards the young doctors who were busy with patients. He said, "Our house officers and interns are a very enthusiastic bunch of upcoming medical professionals. You can expect good support from them."

"Thanks! I will need it tonight," she said.

"And here, I present myself. If you need any help, I am around!"

"Thank you!" she said nodding her head yet again in affirmation.

He then noticed her eyes: glistening, dark eyes, that were so deep and beautiful, yet so distant. Something was missing from them. Something he couldn't put his finger on, as of now. Intriguing. He wondered if it was her newness to the place, a hesitation that had made her look like that. It seemed she had created a wall around her that conveniently allowed her to maintain distance from everyone.

Embarrassed by his flow of thoughts, Aakash then hurriedly proceeded to the next patient. *Why am I so intrigued? What is it about her that is making me so curious?* He was probably one of the last people on earth to be infatuated to anyone. Known for his 'I don't care' attitude, his arrogance ran parallel to his academic records and competence.

The night was indeed a nightmare with an unending list of patients combined with the shortage of paramedical staff. It was bad enough for Avni to commence in a new hospital on emergency duty and the chaos only compounded her woes. She knew that this was not an unusual situation and being in medical practice, she could expect the unexpected. She took a deep breath and tried to calm herself down. There were diagnoses to be made, investigations to be ordered, emergencies to be managed and amongst all this, frayed nerves of patients' relatives to be soothed. Acutely aware of the situation she was in, she started seeing the patients.

She was still busy with a teenage girl when Dr Sandeep informed her about the arrival of a new patient, Mr Singh. Sandeep had already completed his initial evaluation, but felt that the patient needed her immediate attention. After advising the girl's parents for hospital admission, Avni went on to see Mr Singh. The patient seemed to be in his early forties. He was accompanied by four or five people. Avni assumed that they might be his family members. She wanted to tell them not to crowd the emergency, but preferred to remain silent. Avni quickly took the medical history and proceeded to examine him. But before she could begin auscultating using her stethoscope, the patient suddenly started gasping for air. In no time, he had turned blue and fainted.

For a split moment, she froze. No, this was not the way she wanted to start her residency program, her new innings at the hospital, her new life! But instantly she took control of herself. She ordered blood arterial gas estimation and asked the house officer to arrange for oxygen. As it turned out, there were no paramedical staffs around, and by the time the oxygen cylinder was organized in the commotion, the patient passed away.

What followed next was something that was unimaginable to her. The relatives started shouting and abusing aggressively. Soon they were throwing things around – chairs, tables, medical equipment, whatever they could lay their hands on.

"The doctor has not seen my brother properly. Why did she need to repeat the same questions that the other doctor had already asked?" One of them pointed the finger at her and shouted. His flushed face and bloodshot eyes shook Avni to the core, but she tried to keep her nerves under control. In the meanwhile, the other people accompanying the patient thrashed the paramedical staff who was trying to fix the oxygen cylinder. The nurses and other staff scurried for safety as a mini-ruckus ensued. The other patients and their relatives watched in horror as pandemonium unfolded in front of them.

Avni stood there, shocked, her feet trembling with fear. A chill ran down her spine. She tried to speak, but nothing came out of her mouth except a faint sigh. She decided to move, but it was like she was glued to the ground. Her mind went blank. It was just not possible for her to believe that she was being held responsible for someone's death. How could it be? She did whatever was possible at the time. As she tried to force her thoughts back into some semblance of order, she felt a little jerk. Before she could realize, someone caught her by the hand and pulled her away from the middle. At around the same time, security guards also arrived at the scene. Avni turned around to see who had pulled her. But he was already gone. She looked over her shoulder and saw him walking briskly towards the patient's relatives who were still standing there, enraged and resentful. Unmistakably, it was Dr Aakash. Not someone you could forget easily, however little the interaction. He took charge as he began talking to relatives and was seen to be placating them in his own inimitable style. Silently she admired his bearing, efficient and so dignified. His appearance on the scene, just in time, stopped the ruckus from turning into a calamity.

Avni looked in his direction again. He was now trying to calm a woman, who was crying inconsolably. *Maybe she was the wife of the patient who just died.* She took a deep breath. It must be so painful, she squirmed at the thought. She wished if she could offer her some words of sympathy, but she knew it was not possible. She was the target of their wrath. They would not like to see her.

Under Dr Aakash's supervision, she noticed that things slowly started getting normal. The relatives who were so agitated earlier appeared to calm down. Although still upset, they allowed the patient's body to be collected and sent for autopsy. Avni sighed in relief as she saw them finally leaving the place. With the back of her hand, she slowly wiped away tiny drops of sweat that had accumulated on her forehead even on the chilly winter night. Order was restored under the vigilant eyes of Dr Aakash.

Mission over, his eyes searched for Dr Avni. Dr Aakash was not really unsettled by the unexpected turn of events, for he had seen quite a few cases during his training days, but as a chief medical officer on duty, he also had the responsibility of the staff working under him. He had not witnessed the incident himself, but he wanted to believe in his team. Yet, a small voice in his head tried to caution him. He had never worked with Dr Avni before. How could he be sure of her competence or her interactions with patients? But for now, he decided to keep these thoughts at bay.

He found her standing at the back of the room, staring down at the ground beneath, precisely at the same place where he had left her after pulling her out from the ruckus.

"Dr Avni?" he said.

Avni met his inquiring eyes. It was hard to guess what exactly he was thinking, but she knew that she would have never wanted the episode to happen on the very first day of her work. She would have given anything to avert this. How desperately she had wanted to blend in the crowd, to quietly disappear in the humdrum of the hospital's environment to start a new life. An inconspicuous existence where she could finally dissociate herself from the ruins of her past, a past that she would have given anything to forget. How to let go of the past when it just stays with you in the present – all the time,every moment, just below the surface, depleting your energy, stripping you of your hard-earned strength and breaking you into pieces. She remembered how she had finally decided to break free from it and move on with life. Joining this hospital, a new place of work, a new city was perhaps her bravest attempt to tear away from the wreckage that her life had become.

"Yes sir," she said with much effort, trying to sound confident. It was different that she had never felt so vulnerable.

"Are you okay?" Dr Aakash asked, his professional tone in direct contrast to the melange of emotions he was feeling inside.

"Yes sir," she said, infusing much poise in those hollow words. "I am fine." Her tone indicated otherwise.

"Can you please join us in the staff room?" he asked her. She followed him to the room like an obedient student. On reaching there, she saw other doctors from the unit already there. Dr Aakash then took the centre-stage. Avni quietly settled herself in one corner of the room. Before she could have made any attempt to collect her thoughts, she heard him, "Dr Avni!" She looked up; she saw him looking at her, "I hope you took all precautions while seeing the patient."

"Yes, I did!" she heard herself responding a little too early. "He died even before anything could have been done." She knew that she had not done anything wrong or lacked somewhere in her duty as a doctor, but for Avni, such expeditiousness was out of character. She couldn't believe she had just spoken so confidently. She had succeeded in overcoming her fragility in a way that was unthinkable to her, not so long ago. The demons of her past had left her so vulnerable that she was limping back to normalcy with slow, cautious steps. The carefully constructed façade of aloofness was her only shield for self-defense.

Deep inside her heart, Avni knew this second chance came at a price; a price that she had to pay by making no mistakes. Any hesitation on her part and she would be considered an offender. Avni knew she had to fight it out. She couldn't afford not to. She owed it to that one life she cared for. Him.

"He must have had an underlying condition that complicated his problem," she said looking straight into his eyes. He looked back. Now he could see those eyes more clearly. He couldn't read anything though; they were empty, bereft of any discernible emotion.

"I see," said Dr Aakash equivocally, with a sigh of exasperation escaping his mouth.

"Good!" And then after a pause, he said, "Please be careful in future. Sometimes these relatives can be very dangerous. Your safety is important."

After he finished interrogating her, he addressed the assembled staff of other junior doctors, nurses and paramedics gathered in response to the hurriedly called meeting. "Does anyone have any questions?"

"Sir, can't we refer some patients to other hospitals? We are facing an avalanche here. Some of the patients are not even that sick," the house officer promptly questioned.

"I wish we could do that. But we have orders that no patients should be turned away." Although he tried to sound undaunted, he knew that this was an unreasonable directive.

"This is not right, sir!" Dr Sanjay blurted out.

Dr Aakash looked at him and gave a long, weary sigh. "We are not here to debate this. We are here to treat the patients."

And then, without giving a second glance, he walked away to attend the waiting patients. It was going to be a long night, and he was not oblivious to the fact that as a chief of the unit, the final responsibility for patient care and emergency unit management was his.

Dr Avni kept looking at him from the corner of her eyes till he disappeared from sight. She felt overwhelmed with the way the whole thing had turned out, wondering if it was again her destiny that had brought her here tonight, for there was no reason for her to be at the emergency ward otherwise. Gathering all her strength with a fragile heart, she decided to not let this one mishap dampen her already bruised spirit. Fortunately for her, as well as for the others on duty, the rest of the night passed uneventfully, except for a few critical patients who had to be admitted in an emergency.

2

Armed with her wavering belief and fragile confidence, Avni drove to the hospital the next morning. She had managed to get the position of the registrar amidst so many uncertainties. She couldn't believe her luck when she got the letter confirming her residency position. To know that she would be able to do it in a different city – away from the place that constantly reminded her of unpleasant memories – was like a blessing in disguise. Avni knew she couldn't undo the mistake she had committed, but she was trying desperately to make it a part of her past and to build a new future. Now it was on her to pick up the pieces and create a new life. If not for herself, at least for him.

The rocky terrain of her thought process broke when someone honked at her. She glanced in the rear-view mirror; a taxi was trying to overtake her. A faint smile crossed her face as she gave way; she thought of her attitude which had changed so much over the past couple of years. From someone who wouldn't let anyone overtake her, to someone who slowed down to make way for others without any reservations – she surely had come a long way.

Avni was almost near the hospital parking area when she saw Aakash. He was parking his car. Instinctively, she slowed down. Once he was out of sight, she parked hers and hurriedly walked towards the hospital building. Avni repeated to herself that she hadn't done anything wrong and she would not let anything affect her. And once again, she silently promised to herself that nothing should come between her and the new life that she was trying to carve out for herself.

Avni met the resident team at the entrance of medical wards for the morning rounds. The team was headed by Dr Pandey, head of the unit. During the rounds, they were supposed to review overnight events, new admissions and new scans. It was to be followed by the M&M (or Morbidity and Mortality) conference, a regular weekly meeting in which the senior doctors and residents gathered to review mistakes that had been made and cases that had gone wrong.

Too much of a coincidence! Why couldn't this meeting be on any other day? Her single-minded focus on yesterday's event was broken when Dr Pandey started introducing new registrars to the team – her and Nikhil Singh. She could feel a few eyes looking over her. *Was it because of last night's incident*? Feeling a little disconcerted, Avni lowered her eyes to avoid them.

There were a couple of interesting cases in the round, the ones she had seen for the first time in her medical career. Being in a capital city, this place drew patients from all over India. She knew this would be an excellent experience for her, far better than what could have been possible in her town hometown, Allahabad. *But was it the reason for her to move here? Did she choose to do her residency here for the sole reason of her interest in better prospects in the academic career?* The answer to all these questions was a big NO, and she knew it. She knew that she was just running away from her past.

"I heard there was some commotion in the emergency last night," Dr Pandey adjusted his glasses and spoke to no one in particular when morning rounds were over. "Right?"

"Yes sir, a patient had died, and his relatives created some chaos," Dr Neha Tripathi, the senior registrar replied. "It's not unusual these days. The situation could have gotten worse, but Aakash handled it quite well. He stopped it from getting violent."

"Who was filling in for Prakash from our unit?" His next question put Avni on her guard. So this was it. She realized she couldn't afford to be unconfident.

Trying to look unfazed, she said, "It was me, sir!" She then looked around. All eyes were on her. "I was asked by Dr Kapoor to fill in."

Dr Pandey scratched his forehead as if he was trying to remember something. He said, "But you had barely joined the department. I remember now. You and Nikhil were busy with all the formalities of joining on that day. In fact, you both came to see me as well for the unit posting."

"Yes sir!" Nikhil replied. Avni stood still for some time before breaking her silence.

"Sir, I did everything that I could have done." Avni tried to sound calm, but inwardly she shuddered at the prospects of facing the dreaded question, every time.

"I am sure you must have…." Dr Pandey said as he checked his watch for the M&M meeting. He then asked everyone to join the conference.

The conference room was packed with doctors. It was mandatory for everyone from the medicine department to attend. Although Avni had nothing to worry about, but no one would have wanted their post-graduation course to begin with so much drama and uninvited controversy. She was no different. *You have a knack of landing yourself in problems, entirely avoidable ones at that.* She could almost hear her mother's words ringing in her ears. She looked around and thankfully found a place at the back of the room where she could quickly disappear into the sea of white coats.

Avni briefly glanced around the room. Sanjay was seated in the row ahead. He waved at her. She faintly smiled back in return. The front row was occupied by the senior doctors. She noticed Dr Kapoor sitting in front too. *He could have spared me from the unnecessary mess.* Her eyes then hurriedly scanned the room for the one person she desired to not be there. Strangely, she didn't want him there, but despite her, a part of her secretly wanted him to be there. As if on cue, he, along with Neha Tripathi walked into the packed room. His handsome face looked serious; it was like he was lost in some deep thoughts. His broad shoulders looked as if they were bearing the weight of the whole world. He could comfortably fit into the definition of a Greek God with his well-chiselled, sharp features.

Dr Kapoor welcomed everyone to the meeting. "M&M meeting is now open for case presentations. It will be followed by a discussion," he said, gesturing towards the senior registrars, Aakash and Neha. "Expect a brainstorming session!"

Neha, a petite woman with an eager face and twinkling eyes, took over the podium. Lights were dimmed in the room as she started the PowerPoint presentation from Unit I.

On the screen, the facts and figures were being displayed. Facts that human lives were vulnerable, however much we tend to believe otherwise. That pain and misery were inevitable. That death was the universal truth. However, those very facts also showed that mankind had conquered so many ills. That human spirit was untameable. And then there were figures that tried to confirm those undeniable facts. Most of the statistics regarding admissions, discharges, morbidity & mortality were the usual; however, one patient had died of bacterial meningitis. The adult patient had reported to emergency with symptoms of high fever, neck stiffness and nausea. Due to the ongoing flu epidemic, he was initially suspected to be suffering from the same. He had been admitted, his nasopharyngeal swab taken for PCR diagnosis and was advised to take Tamiflu by Dr Ashwin Gupta, junior registrar of Unit I. But his condition started deteriorating rapidly. He developed a purple-red skin rash and became drowsy and confused. By the time Ashwin ordered a cerebrospinal fluid test suspecting meningitis, the patient had slipped into a coma and later died.

When Neha finished speaking, the lights came back on, and the room brightened up again. Avni squinted to adjust her eyes and looked around.

As per the norm, Dr Kapoor opened the discussion, "The case is now open for discussion. Let me make the first comment." He glanced at Ashwin and added in a grave voice, "I think it was misdiagnosed. You should have been more alert."

"Sir, it was tough to pinpoint the diagnosis of meningitis in the beginning," Ashwin defended himself. "Especially since almost all of the cases admitted in emergency were of flu."

"But you should have at least put meningitis down as a differential diagnosis," Dr Bhatia, Head of Unit II remarked.

Neha was standing silently after presenting the case, and interjected, "Sir, having it as a differential diagnosis wouldn't have changed the initial management. I believe Ashwin didn't flounder anywhere." She gave a reassuring look to Ashwin. "He managed the case as per the requirement. It was only later that the patient developed a rash and altered sensorium."

"And then I immediately ordered for CSF," Ashwin felt a little recharged after getting Neha's support.

"I think he did everything possible. In such a situation, sometimes it's not possible to rule out all causes of high fever in every patient. It might have been easier if it wasn't for the pandemic and it would have been just a regular admission," Dr Pandey scratched his forehead and commented after listening for a while. Avni looked at Ashwin. He heaved a sigh of relief and took his seat. Dr Kapoor preferred to remain silent.

Avni felt her heart racing when Dr Kapoor announced, "Now we will have Unit II presentation." He gestured towards Aakash who promptly took his position and glanced at the assembled crowd before starting the presentation. The light was dimmed again as his deep voice reverberated around the meeting room. Avni glanced at Aakash and he returned her look as passively as a stranger on a bus.

Comprehensively presenting the data with an in-depth analysis of patients and their illnesses, he breezed through the presentation. She tried to find a flaw, any flaw in him that would make him more real. Perfection is so unreal; flaws make us real, she pondered as she listened to him.

Aakash promptly finished his presentation. The room brightened up again as the lights were switched on. There was not much to discuss, everything was fitting into the criteria of good medical practice, *except* one case.

Aakash glanced up at Avni before he spoke again, but his face was blank, his eyes were like closed windows. "We had a case of Mr Singh, a 45-year-old patient who was brought to emergency for suspected flu." Avni felt her face getting flushed. Suddenly last night of madness came alive in front of her eyes.

"Who saw the case in the emergency?" Dr Kapoor asked Aakash.

The moment she had been dreading was here. *What if she was sued for medical malpractice? What if she was debarred from practicing medicine?* But then, she convinced herself that she had done her best and couldn't have done any better. It was not the apprehension of being judged, but fear of being dragged into unnecessary drama at the start of her new career, a new life. The perturbation was not for her life but for him; her most treasured possession.

"Dr Avni Trivedi," he said; his professional tone betraying the scepticism that he couldn't resist feeling about the case

"Can Dr Avni explain the case in detail?" Dr Kapoor said, looking in her direction.

Before she could reply, Prakash, the senior registrar of Unit I who was on leave on that fateful day and was replaced by Avni spoke, "I would like to make a comment before you begin, Dr Avni." He looked around at the junior doctors. "I have heard from other doctors that relatives of the patient were very volatile. They were abusing everyone who was present there." Looking at Dr Kapoor, he continued, "Sir, the safety of doctors is as important as that of the patient's health, if not more. If not for Dr Aakash, things would have gone out of control. The hospital needs to ensure the safety of its doctors."

Dr Kapoor's dark brows drew together in a frown. "Of course, that goes without saying. I will ensure that security around the hospital is upgraded."

"I am sure Dr Kapoor would look into that, but this being an M&M meeting, we must first discuss Mr Singh's case," Aakash interrupted. Then he looked in her direction, "Dr Avni..." He was cool and courteous, his neutral tone in direct contrast to her shock and trepidation. "I hope you can shed some light on the case."

For a split second, her eyes were locked with his. For the first time, since he had met her, he could see something other than emptiness in them. Irritation? Frustration? Anger? Pain? Or just plain indifference? He couldn't decide.

"First of all, let me thank Dr Aakash. He took great care of the situation." She glanced at Aakash. He wondered if she was being sarcastic, but he couldn't find any echo of his suspicion in her voice. Every word spoken was deliberate, calm and measured.

"Now coming to the case," she looked at Dr Kapoor who was keenly observing her response. Perhaps in the process, he was also trying to judge his own decision of posting a newbie in the emergency ward, at a time when there was an ongoing pandemic situation. Although Aakash had given him feedback the day before, he wanted to hear it from her; her side of the story.

Avni recounted the incident in as much detail as possible. From the arrival of the patient to his death, everything happened so quickly that it was almost impossible to stretch the details to more than ten minutes. But she didn't want to take any chances. Any loophole could allow them to point fingers at her. She had to defend herself.

"So you did everything possible at the time to care for the patient?" Dr Kapoor asked.

"Yes sir!" she replied, "I also ordered for oxygen when the patient started gasping for breath."

"No one is denying the fact that you took care of the patient when he started gasping. The question is if there was any delay in starting the treatment," Aakash interrupted. It was like he wanted to visualize precisely what all happened before the patient died. For him, it didn't matter if it was Avni on duty or anyone else. She glanced at him. It was almost comical, primarily because she was in the midst of a storm in her professional life, but she wondered, *how he would have looked without this permanent frown on his face.*

She spoke slowly this time, pausing between each word so he could understand what he wanted to know.

"As far as I am concerned, there was no delay. Although I wanted to confirm what the intern had told me about the patient, he collapsed when I had barely started to ask." She looked around, her eyes resting on the intern who was present with her at that time. "You can confirm with Sandeep and also with a nurse on duty, Miss Nisha, who were around at that time."

Her defiance startled him. He never expected her to be so confident, so sure about herself. If he had met her a couple of years ago, he might have found an unsure, vulnerable girl, but not anymore. She had learned the hard way, and there was no way she was going to unlearn it just because of someone's idiosyncrasy.

He looked at her. She was removing strands of hair from her face. She looked so pretty with her flushed cheeks and dark eyes, looking lost in some deep thought. Although she was wearing the doctor's coat, it didn't stop her slim figure from forming a perfect silhouette on the wall behind her. Feeling embarrassed with himself for looking at her a little longer than necessary, he swiftly shifted his gaze. He had been convinced that there was a critical delay in the treatment, which had proved to be fatal for the patient.

He shrugged his shoulders. "I still feel that patient could have been saved."

Avni could not help herself from comparing him with the other senior registrars. *Dr Neha was so protective of her junior. She defended him at every step. And here was a senior registrar who was hell-bent on deeming her guilty*. However, she remained unfazed.

"The autopsy report will be available soon. I believe the patient had some pre-existing clinical condition that led to his death." Her voice had a kind of authority, an unintended determination that surprised her too. *So she could pretend how strong she was.*

"I agree with Dr Avni. She has a very valid point. We can wait for the autopsy report." Dr Pandey, the Unit I head, who was sitting silently until now, spoke. Removing his glasses, he looked at Dr Kapoor, "We should be cautious in posting a new registrar in the emergency ward. She had just joined in the morning. She had no idea about working in the hospital. Feasibly, an experienced registrar was needed in such conditions." He felt that Aakash was unnecessarily holding the girl responsible, and that too, without any valid proof.

She was in his Unit, and he had to be unbiased. He had taught Aakash and had also worked with him. It wasn't any secret that he was a perfectionist, who at times, was too hard on others. He had undoubtedly inherited the trait from his father who was known to be a terror in medical school until he resigned to start his own medical practice. Thankfully, the son was a mutant, not as dangerous as his father, he thought to himself.

"Thank you for your advice, Dr Pandey!" Although Dr Kapoor was a little unsettled by the strong opinion he had about the registrar's postings, but he didn't show it. "We will be careful in future. Further, we will wait for the autopsy report before making a final call on the situation." He then looked at Dr Prakash, "Also, we will ensure better security for our doctors."

Soon after, the meeting ended.

Avni caught Aakash looking at her as she collected her stuff when their eyes met again for a split second. They looked steadily at each other for a moment and then away again; she nonchalantly and he grudgingly. She wondered if her old self would have smiled back at him and whispered in his ears what she had read somewhere, "*Don't take yourself so seriously; no one else does.*"

Soon enough, both of them left the hall through different exits.

3

"The autopsy report of that patient is out…what was his name?" Nikhil asked Avni. "I forgot…."

"Mr Singh, you mean?" she asked.

"Yes. The one Aakash was getting so paranoid about," he said in a sarcastic tone. "It's now available with Dr Kapoor."

Avni didn't say anything. She was busy with a patient suffering from aortic stenosis. Briefly, she wanted to leave the patient and find out the details of the autopsy findings, but she resisted. She was not here to prove any point or to have any sort of competition with anyone. Worse still, she didn't believe in settling scores with Aakash. Although she was taken aback yesterday, was a little upset also, but she wanted to forget about the whole thing. She was here to complete her degree. To reclaim the life that was bruised because of her recklessness. How different it would've been if she was prudent in her approach towards life. Her mother's words kept echoing in her ears, "*You have a tendency to make the wrong choices.*" She could not afford to let go of this opportunity to redeem herself. However difficult her life had become, but she had one thing that had given her enough strength to fight back. She could not let him down.

The patient of aortic stenosis, a twenty-five-year-old male, had a history of rheumatic fever and had been admitted with chest pain and shortness of breath. She ordered an ECG and cardiac catheterization to evaluate the severity. Once she was done with the patient, she walked to the doctor's room.

"Sorry, Nikhil! I couldn't talk to you before..." she said as she entered the room.

"No problem, Dr Avni! I understand. It was just that I feel it was unjust to accuse you of the patient's death." He closed the book he was reading and stood up. "I just wanted to give you the good news."

"So you know about the report?" Clearly surprised, Avni was curious.

"No big deal, Dr Avni. Why are you so surprised?" He smiled. "I have a friend who is doing his registrarship in the forensic department. He told me about it." Nikhil was enjoying that he had privileged information through which he could garner Avni's undivided attention.

"First, stop calling me Dr Avni. You can call me Avni. I am your batchmate."

As soon as she mouthed those words, she felt that she once again belonged to the familiar environment of the medical school. The tension, the fun, the fantastic life of medical school was beckoning her again. It was as if she had never left all this behind. She felt light without her cloak of aloofness that she had donned to hide her real self.

She smiled. "Well, tell me about the report."

Nikhil was enjoying her undivided attention. "The patient died because of pre-existing chronic obstructive lung disease (COPD).

Flu had only aggravated his condition," he said. "It was nothing to do with you."

She felt a massive sense of relief.

"Let's see what Aakash has to say now!" Nikhil said with a glee on his face. She felt relieved that at least she would be finally absolved, but strangely, she didn't particularly enjoy Nikhil's sarcastic remark about Aakash. She just responded for the sake of it; a faint smile that had no echoes in her eyes. *If not for this uninvited controversy, she would have nothing to do with Aakash; she wanted to stay clear of anything that was not in sync with her new life. She had learned that smiling was the best way to avoid saying anything obvious. She prized herself with the thought of how entirely she had been able to transform herself from a talkative, ever cheerful girl to an aloof and enigmatic woman. Not a bad job, after all. Life had indeed been the best teacher.*

Failing to get an interesting response from her, he continued, "It seems Dr Kapoor is calling a meeting in the afternoon. The two unit heads are also supposed to attend. Perhaps you might also be called to attend besides Aakash." Then he laughed again, a little mischievously this time, "In the meantime, I did my own little research on Aakash."

"What?" She looked at him baffled. "Why would you do something like that?"

"Don't be shocked. It might help you to deal with Aakash in a better way." He then looked around, as if to check if anyone was listening. Then he almost whispered, "He has inherited a lot from his father. He is a kind of a miniature version of him. A little terrorist from the staff's point of view, but a brilliant, committed doctor to his patients. And I have heard that he feels deeply for them," Nikhil paused for a while. He then continued, "Perhaps that's the reason he is after the Singh case."

'*To feel things deeply*.' She couldn't decide if that was good or bad.

"And one more interesting fact about him, besides his professional life..." He articulated with his eyes gleaming.

She looked at him enquiringly. "Do I need to know that?"

"Depends on how you would like to process that piece of information," he added with an impish look on his face. "He has a reputation of being quite popular with the ladies. But apparently, he keeps his professional and personal life strictly separate, in two different watertight compartments."

Avni was walking back from the cafeteria after lunch when her mobile buzzed. It was a message from Dr Kapoor's office asking her to attend a meeting at 2.30 p.m. Avni tried to finish her work before the meeting as she hated going home late in the evening. She compiled the list of patients with HIV/AIDS attending the hospital in the current week for the follow-up.

When she rechecked her watch, it was already 2.30 p.m. She hurriedly walked across the corridor to the HOD office. On hearing the sound of her footsteps, the secretary, Miss Priya looked up from the computer screen, "Oh doctor! You are here. Everyone is waiting for you," she said.

Avni leaped to the door that led to Dr Kapoor's room. She could feel her palms getting sweaty. Slowly she opened the door to enter the room while taking deep breaths. She looked around the room. Dr Pandey and Dr Bhatia were also present besides the head, Dr Kapoor. Her eyes then caught Aakash who was sitting in the far corner. He avoided looking at her. He was wearing glasses today, which gave him an intellectual look. He was looking at nothing in particular. For a second, his blank stare confounded her. Sitting amongst them all, somehow he seemed so lonely. She wondered if one had to pay the price of being too driven, to the point of being obsessive. Or was it something else.

As Dr Kapoor offered Avni a seat, Aakash finally looked at her. She looked back. There was so much to say, and then there was nothing to say.

"The autopsy report is now available. The patient had a long history of COPD." His eyes travelled to Aakash who was listening to every word attentively.

"Oh! That means flu just precipitated the pre-existing condition. It wasn't the cause of his death," Dr Pandey said.

"In any case, even without any pre-existing condition, he could have died of flu," Dr Bhatia spoke slowly in between coughing, "Dr Avni shouldn't have been held responsible for his death."

"No one was holding her responsible; we were waiting for the report." Dr Kapoor looked at Aakash.

"I still believe Dr Avni could have been more prompt." Aakash's arrogance was raw; unabashed and unrepentant.

Avni listened to what he had just said and sighed. She wanted to let go of it. Let go of the senseless drama she was being sucked into. "Dr Aakash, I respect your sentiments. I respect that you are a very committed doctor. But having said that, I must remind you that we are only doctors, we are not god!" She glanced at all the three professors sitting there. "Sometimes, in spite of our best efforts, we can't do anything." Neither did she blame him, nor did she bring up the findings of the autopsy report. Avni was just matter of fact as she didn't want a new enemy when she was not sure if she was even done with the old ones.

"Well, that could be your opinion Dr Avni, not mine." He almost snapped.

Dr Kapoor silently watched the scene unfold in front of him, feeling a little guilty for posting Dr Avni in emergency on her very first day. "I think the autopsy report is unequivocal. There should be no doubt about the cause of the patient's death." He looked at Dr Aakash, "It's good that you are so concerned about the patients, but I guess it would be unfair to judge Dr Avni based on one incident."

4

Ever since Avni had joined the new hospital, this was the first weekend she could actually put her feet up and relax, away from work; especially after the eventful week. She always loved to spend her spare time at home as that meant spending it with her most treasured possession – her six-month-old son, Vivan. It was bliss to be around him. With his innocent laughter ringing aloud in the house, she forgot all her pain and worries. One look at his angelic face ensured she slept peacefully. His twinkling eyes were a sight to the sore eyes.

Mrs Joseph was preparing to give him a bath. Avni was fortunate to have found such a caring nanny who could look after Vivan better than her own self. In a new city, with no relatives and just a handful of acquaintances, Mrs Joseph was like a blessing. Just because of her, Avni could do her residency away from home.

"Be careful! sometimes kids can drown in the bathtub in a matter of seconds. Keep watching him," Mrs Joseph called out in a loud voice from the kitchen when she realized that Avni was going to give a bath to Vivan.

"Okay, I will," Avni said. *Mrs Joseph has become so possessive about Vivan. She smiled to herself. She doesn't even trust me, his own mother.*

Every day, Vivan jumped with joy as soon as she arrived from work, wanting to be hugged immediately. Avni also longed to cuddle him and hold the centre of her universe in her arms. But Mrs Joseph would have none of it until Avni had showered and changed into her pajamas. "Don't get the baby infected with your hospital bugs." Avni didn't mind. She could bet on her with Vivan's life. Mrs Joseph loved him like her own child, going to any extent to make him happy and comfortable. Mrs Joseph was in her mid-fifties, almost the same age as her mother. But it was just there that similarities ended.

Her own mother could never bring herself to love Vivan the way Mrs Joseph did. She could never forgive Avni for marrying against their wishes; bringing disappointment and sorrow that she had never imagined even in her worst nightmares. Her father, Mr Trivedi was no different, but at least Avni was spared of his anger as he never interacted with her after that fateful day. He just stopped talking to her. He didn't know any other way; he was never good at scolding his children or hiding his feelings with empty words. However, his silence killed her more than her mother's outward show of displeasure. *At least her mother felt lighter by venting out her anger, but what about him?* He had retracted into a shell, a shell that was getting hardened by the weight of his own unhappiness.

Avni knew that they would never like her husband, that he could never be a suitable boy in their eyes, that they would never accept him as their son-in-law.

But somehow she was vaguely confident that the birth of a child would change everything, that they wouldn't hold back their love for the baby. After all, he would be their first grandchild. She remembered the day Vivan was born. How she held him in her arms and inspected him like a much-cherished gift. She counted his fingers, his toes. She stared at his gorgeous face for so long. She was ecstatic. Everything was just perfect. She silently thanked god for being so kind. She could never forget the moment when he had opened his eyes for the first time. Her whole world had seemed to stop. She looked unblinkingly into those eyes and for the first time in her life, found her worthiness. Her heart was filled with a kind of love that was yet unknown to her. And then a sudden, deep realization occurred to her; the realization that now she was responsible for another life, and she couldn't afford to fail him. She felt her eyes getting moist. At that very moment, she made a promise to herself. No matter what, she would never let him down. He deserved to be loved unconditionally, irrespective of anything that she was going through.

Her husband came to see them much later, when she had already dozed off after such an exhausting day. On finding her asleep, he left soon after, just having a quick glimpse of their baby. The nurse informed her about it as she woke her up around two in the morning to feed the baby. The only other family member present at the delivery was her sister-in-law who was there more as a formality rather than any emotional connect. She left as soon as Avni was shifted to her hospital suite from the labor room. And her parents, Mr and Mrs Trivedi never came to see their first grandchild at the hospital.

Avni looked at her son. He was playing with the newspaper, cooing with delight for being able to lay his hands on one. For him, the humble newspaper was more precious than any of his expensive toys which he would promptly dump to catch the paper in his tiny hands and feet. It was almost an everyday ritual; the rustling sound that papers made against each other seemed like music to his ears, Avni thought. It filled her heart with so much joy. Vivan was her mirror image. She was strangely relieved that he didn't look like his father, not one bit. It was easier for her to forget him; a constant reminder of something one wants to forget was not her idea of overcoming the past. At least it spared her from the painful and unpleasant memories.

Avni again glanced at her infant son and felt that perhaps it was all worth it. Whatever happened to her marriage, she could bring life into existence. She cherished these moments of pure bliss. It had only been six months since he came into this world, but to her, it seemed that she had been with him forever. She had always known him, perhaps from some other time, some different universe.

Her reverie was broken by a call from her younger sister, Sia, her only real friend in this world. She was also the bridge, the primary source of communication with her parents. Her father still didn't talk to her while her mother maintained a cautious, grudging distance, where she did her duty, but reserved her love as a mother. Not that Avni complained about it, conceivably they were right. If not in the beginning, ironically they were later proven right. At times she wondered, if it was their curse that the boy they disliked indeed confirmed to their suspicions in the course of time. But somehow she couldn't bring herself to believe it, especially after becoming a mother herself, for parents could never think poorly for their child.

5

It was Monday. Avni was getting ready for the hospital after settling Vivan, who was a little cranky this morning. She quickly glanced in the mirror, and for a moment, she couldn't stop herself from admiring her own image. It was hard to tell that she was a mother now. She was back in shape after Vivan's birth so soon. She could fit into her old dresses, even from her graduation days. Her stomach looked as flat as in her younger days; her face also as fresh and innocent. But then, a sudden feeling of overwhelming regret gripped her. It was like her own reflection in the mirror had opened the floodgate of disappointments, of marrying him against almost every possible logic, of the years lost in the aftermath of turmoil, and the worst regret of all – of losing her own self in search of his validation.

She stood staring at the mirror a little longer than she could afford with her time, wishing ludicrously if she could rewind the clock. The pain that she had kept buried, consciously, with all her efforts, again reared its ugly head at that moment – the dark pain of humiliation, the searing pain of being deceived, the pain of being an enabler for she allowed it to happen; the worst kind of pain where she knew that she had failed herself more than anyone else. Vivan's innocent face flashed in her mind and then once again she knew that she needed immense strength to make new beginnings.

She waved to Vivan and Mrs Joseph as she started the engine of her car, a new Toyota sedan, the only luxury that she had allowed herself to possess after moving to Delhi. It was going to be a busy day. Mondays always were. Besides attending the OPD in the morning, she had to take care of her own patients; patients that were enrolled for her dissertation. She could not afford to be lax about the thesis like the other residents who had recently joined the course with her. They had ample time to do the work. She didn't. With her son growing up, she would need more time for him.

Avni was about to step into the full OPD block when she bumped into Nikhil Singh. He was coming from the main department.

"Did you hear the great news?" he said.

"What news?"

"Perhaps you won't like it!" he said with a cheeky smile.

"Tell me. You don't need to worry if I like it or not."

"Ok! So brace yourself for the storm."

She was now looking concerned. She thought that something had come up again regarding the death of Mr Singh.

"Dr Aakash is now posted in Unit II, our unit." He looked at her. With her eyebrows furrowed together, she looked perplexed. She looked so pretty even when her face was contorted, he thought.

"The registrars have been reshuffled; the new duty roster has been released today. Dr Neha is now posted in Unit I," he said.

"I see," she said briefly and Nikhil was left wondering at the ambiguity of her response.

Although Avni could easily hide her feelings from Nikhil, she couldn't hide it from herself; she came face to face with an uninvited wave of frustration and anger. If she had a choice, she wouldn't have wanted anything to do with Aakash. He might have been an overzealous, committed doctor; but she would have been happier without having him supervise her on an everyday basis. For now, she had her own demons to fight, she didn't want any battle with the outside world. *But since when did life let you opt out of its unpredictable, unscheduled tests because you wanted to?*

"Well, thanks for the information." She forced herself to smile. "I have to rush to Dr Pandey's OPD. I'll see you later."

She then hurriedly rushed towards room number 4 of the OPD.

Avni was relieved to see that Dr Pandey hadn't arrived yet, but felt guilty when she noticed that patients were already waiting. She knew that even in this cold winter, patients would queue up early in the morning to get an appointment.

It was her first day at the OPD as a registrar, and she didn't want to take any chances. Although she could have dismissed the uncomplicated cases after seeing the patient and prescribing medication, she preferred to wait for Dr Pandey to see all those cases as well. In her mind, she thought that gradually she would only keep the intricate, complex cases for him, but for now, it was best to have all cases reviewed by him, as advised to the new registrars during their orientation on the first day.

It was already more than an hour, but still, there was no sign of Dr Pandey. It was a little unusual as generally the clinic was informed well in advance if any consultant was late or absent. Avni asked the nurse to call the medicine department to check what was going on. She was returning to the OPD room after talking to the nurse when she heard someone walking behind her with brisk steps. Out of curiosity, she looked over her shoulder.

Dr Aakash Mehta! *What is he doing here?* In the midst of so much of work, she had forgotten what Nikhil had told her earlier, that Aakash was now posted in Unit II. She was still contemplating as to how to avoid him without making it visible when she heard him calling her name in his characteristically deep voice, "Dr Avni..."

She turned around to look at the person she so wanted to avoid. For a moment their eyes met, but then Avni instantly looked away to evade his.

"Dr Pandey is not well." Avni then heard him, speaking in the crisp, professional tone. She looked back at him again.

"I am filling in for him," he said. "You are the junior registrar posted with Dr Pandey, I think?"

"That's right," she said in an equally professional tone.

"Well then, let's start with the job. I assume you have already started seeing the patients," he said as he entered the out-patient room. She followed him.

"Yes, Dr Aakash." Avni was now standing facing him. "I was waiting for Dr Pandey to review all the cases. I have done the work-up of around twenty patients." She gestured towards the pile of files lying on the table. "Still there are a lot more to follow, but you can start seeing the already worked-up ones."

There was not even an iota of hesitation or suppressed resentment in her voice; no remnant of their past 'not so good' interactions. She remembered how her father used to tell her when she had joined the MBBS course. "Whatever happens, always be compassionate to your patients. They come first. You have chosen a very noble profession. You should maintain its dignity."

Once the formalities of handing over the charge to Dr Aakash were completed, she resumed seeing the new patients who were waiting for her. Despite a part of him not wanting to, he threw a glance at her; she was looking much younger than the last time they had met. She was looking at ease, entirely different from the day when he saw her for the first time in the emergency ward. Her poise, the graceful way in which she was dealing with patients, made her look all the more charming.

"Dr Avni, can I talk to you for a moment?" She must have been working on her third case when she heard him. His voice had an unmistakable edge to it.

"Sure."

Oh god! Not again. She slowly moved in between the jostling crowd of the patients to face him.

"I wonder why you have chosen to keep such simple cases for me to review. Patients with fever, cough and diarrhea can easily be seen by just you." He raised his eyes from the stacked up files to look at her. "Besides keeping the patients waiting unnecessarily, it crowds the outpatient clinic."

She could feel a sense of irritation in his voice. She was also aware of the patients who were waiting there, keenly observing them.

"As a new registrar, this is what we have been told to do," she said, her tone very matter of fact again, devoid of or any reaction to his unnecessary annoyance. She wondered what made him think that things would work according to his wishes rather than hospital rules. *He must be aware of the rules.*

"I see!" Although he resisted from making any further comment, he felt all the more irritated with her cold response. Both of then proceeded with their respective tasks with heavy silence hanging thick in the air between them until almost at the end of the OPD when a woman in her thirties with symptoms of severe anemia arrived there. Avni did the initial work-up and then sent her to be reviewed by Dr Aakash. He was about to leave as OPD hours were over when he saw the patient, wheeled into his cubicle. Instantly, just one look at the patient and he knew that there was something seriously wrong with her. She looked pale, almost white. He glanced at the history and examination reports prepared by Dr Avni. He then checked all the investigations she had advised for. Nothing seemed to be amiss, but somehow he had a nagging doubt about her condition. She just didn't seem to merely be a case of anemia. He suspected her of having some cardiac complications. He examined her. His suspicion was right. She had an irregular heartbeat and shortness of breath. He immediately advised her husband for admission. He asked Avni to complete the formalities. She promptly did what she was told, but she could feel something was amiss, merely by looking at his expression.

"Dr Avni." Although half expecting it, she was startled when she heard him calling her name. It was already 1 p.m., well past the usual OPD closing time and she was finishing all the pending tasks before leaving for lunch.

"Yes, Dr Aakash." She turned to look at him.

"Can you please come here?" He impatiently pointed towards the patient's file. "I need to discuss something."

She walked up to him in slow, deliberate steps. *What now? Why he is getting so worked up?*

"Did you auscultate the patient?" he asked brusquely.

"Yes," she said. For the first time, she felt a little nervous.

"Didn't you find anything abnormal? The patient has an arrhythmia. She could progress to heart failure if left untreated."

"I did order an ECG," she said in a low voice.

"That's okay. But not everything needs to be diagnosed by investigations. You should be able to pick up the signs and symptoms while examining the patient." He was relentless.

"Yes. I should have picked it up. I am sorry!" She stared at the floor, not making any excuses.

He was expecting anything but an apology. There was a moment of silence. *If your enemy already accepts his defeat, what else is left for you to say? He wondered where her defiance was gone. He had wanted to argue with her, shout at her. To feel vindicated that he had proved her to be careless.* Little did he know how wrong he was! How he had misunderstood her!

"Be careful in the future. You are dealing with human lives."

She kept standing there for some time. *Lonely? Sad? Disappointed? Humiliated? Was he unfair to her? Does he have to show her down every time?* But somehow she found that the answer to all the questions was a big NO. *It was her mistake. She was here to learn. Errors are a part of the learning process, her father used to say when she had trouble memorizing multiplication tables in elementary school.*

Still, Avni couldn't make sense of his unreasonable vexation. It couldn't merely be a coincidence that whenever they worked together, he had an issue with her. If it were in the earlier days, she would have given him a piece of her mind, without bothering if he was senior to her. She would have been his perfect match by being as arrogant, as angry as him, but not anymore. She now wanted to avoid unnecessary confrontation at any cost until and unless she was pushed into the corner. Time and experience had humbled her. Her aloofness was now a façade to avoid any undesired interactions. Her indifference provided her the insulation from the world, protection from ever getting hurt again. Little did she know that it was her very aloofness that aggravated Dr Aakash! It offended his sensibilities, questioned his supremacy, and challenged his beliefs.

6

It was Delhi Medical School and Hospital's annual day celebration. During the day, an exhibition on lifestyle diseases had been organized for the general public. Avni was in-charge at one of the pavilions, where school children were being taught about healthy habits in daily life. She enjoyed interacting with young ones.

As a kid herself, she could only see the glamorous part of being a doctor. She could never imagine how difficult it was to become one. She felt good, proud of herself that she could actualize her childhood dream. Soon after marriage, her then-husband ensured that every accomplishment of hers got trivialized. She was never good enough in his eyes, and gradually, even she had started believing him. She doubted herself. She sought his approval for every small thing; be it her appearance, or her actions, knowing well that she was never going to get any. But it was something that she couldn't help. Sometimes, however much you know the outcome of an action you are propelled toward doing it anyway. Perhaps that was because of her hope. Her desperate hope, however, didn't survive for long and somewhere along with that she lost her self-worth too. The worth that she was now trying to regain.

A cultural program was scheduled for the evening, and Avni decided not to attend it. She had to go home to Vivan. It was impossible for her to think about anything else, least of all a cultural evening.

Avni drove back home. In the six months of his life, she had never left him alone in the evenings. However, setting aside her doubts, she finally decided to attend the cultural evening. Avni said to Mrs Joseph, "I don't really want to, but I think I have to go."

Mrs Joseph nodded. "That's good! You should go. I can take care of Vivan."

Avni chose to wear a salmon pink saree, a gift from a childhood friend on her wedding day. It was a pure silk saree with a delicate silver border. She looked ravishing; her complexion glowed in its reflection. She left her hair open with curls falling over her shoulders. It was after ages that she was getting ready for any occasion. She had forgotten she could ever look beautiful. Her then-husband had always made her feel so inferior. She had lost all her confidence in herself. It didn't take long for her hopes and dreams to shatter. Before she could realize, she was facing the cruel reality of her marriage. But somehow after so many years, today as she recollected those memories without feeling sad. She couldn't help feeling proud of herself for she had come to a long distance from the days when her painful past would just be below the surface, ready to simmer anytime and singe her with its flames.

When Avni reached the venue, the event was about to begin. A vast crowd had gathered at the auditorium with everyone jostling for space. For a moment, she wanted to give it a miss and return to her small world that was so comfortable and familiar. But before she could have cemented her thoughts and made plans to turn back, Nikhil and Sanjay appeared on the scene. They could have never expected such a change in her appearance, from a plain Jane to such a glamorous avatar, but none of them said anything except perhaps admiring inwardly

Then all three of them slowly made their way through the crowded auditorium.

Few vacant seats in the second row had been reserved for the registrars from the Medicine unit. Avni wanted to sink deep in the chair and disappear, away from the glare and blaze, wondering why she was there. She was distracted by the comedy skit being held on stage. It was a comedy about arguments between a husband and wife. People all around were clapping and laughing. Following the skit, the announcement was made about the next act – a ghazal by Dr Aakash Mehta. She glanced sideways at Nikhil, her eyebrows drawn together in a furrow and eyes curious with probably hundreds of questions.

She whispered to him, "Does he sing also?" she said.

"He does," Nikhil said. "He is supposed to be an excellent singer. He has this unusual, haunting voice. This guy is an all-rounder."

"I just can't believe it." She found it intriguing that such a rude person could also have a softer side.

Soon enough, Dr Aakash was on stage donning a casual looking pair of jeans and white shirt, looking as dapper as always. He looked around, holding the mike, scanning the crowd as judiciously as he watched over his patients. He then tested his mike a couple of times, and was about to start singing when he raised his eyes once again; this was when he noticed her, sitting in the second row, almost invisible in her chair. For a moment, his eyes remained fixed on her before he looked away. Avni couldn't precisely define how she felt at that particular moment; she couldn't deduce anything from those bright, transparent eyes, but for that split moment everything stopped. There was nothing that existed beyond it. And then, that moment ceased to exist without even a trace as he started singing.

His voice was so captivating. Girls went crazy. Avni had never seen such a crazy fan following, at least not in a medical school. Her eyes secretly followed him as he left the stage and after he was gone, she kept looking at the empty stage for some time.

7

Today also, just like every other day, by the time Aakash got home, his parents had gone off to sleep. He poured himself a glass of wine and made himself comfortable on the big couch. It was Saturday night, and he was not on call the next day, so he could afford to get up late in the morning. Switching on the TV, he noticed that the European soccer league match was on, which he kept watching till his eyes were heavy with sleep. With much effort, he crawled into bed. And then the recurring nightmare came to haunt him again. That he was alone and lost somewhere, falling into a deep abyss. He was calling out, but there was no one around to help him. When he thought he was about to die, he opened his eyes and found himself covered in sweat, relieved that it wasn't real. It was just a dream, or perhaps some deep-seated insecurity in the form of a dream? He couldn't decide. He got up, had a glass of water and then went back to sleep.

For Dr Avni, Sunday was not a rest day. She wanted to spend her day with her precious baby, but she couldn't. On Monday, she had her first thesis work presentation on HIV/AIDS. She had started collecting data from the very beginning of her posting. The presentation was to be attended by the entire faculty as well as fellows and registrars. Nikhil was also presenting. He was joking the day before about how unprepared he was in comparison to her. It had been three months since they had joined and he had hardly paid any attention to his thesis work. Avni did not want to leave anything till the last minute, for any surprise could be in store for a mother of a young baby

Avni collected her car keys to go to the hospital library. She knew that it would be impossible to do her last minute preparation at home with Vivan around. Somehow, however small he was, he had an inclination of her holiday schedule, the days when Vivaan would just want to be with her all day long. He would love to be taken for a stroll in the nearby park instead of being nestled in the safety of his home with Mrs Joseph.

Mrs Joseph was holding Vivan in her arms. But as soon as he saw Avni picking the keys, he threw open his arms in her direction in anticipation of the car ride to the park. Instead, she waved him goodbye with a heavy heart and went out of the door. She heard him crying loudly, but she decided not to turn back. She knew if she did, she wouldn't be able to go. And she had to go; if not for her, then for his sake. It was a silent promise to do anything and everything for giving him a better life; that she would never let him feel the void created by his father's absence. She didn't want to live with the guilt that she deprived her son of a comfortable life and hence had decided to open her own clinic after finishing her residency.

The library was full of students, residents and fellows. She quietly settled in the study area and went through her data. She had some data in place, and she was sure that she would be able to get all the missing information. At the end of almost six hours of non-stop work, at around 5 p.m., she decided to call it a day. Tired and hungry, she left for home.

On the way back, she thought about how her father always wanted her to finish her post-graduation before getting married. She had openly defied him by marrying Samir Verma, who had blinded her with the promise of undying love. For her, the world stopped at him; nothing else mattered until the day when it all came crashing down. *How terrible it was. How did she manage to survive it?* For a second, she felt proud of herself, of being a struggling survivor rather than being a victim. Her registrarship was also a chapter in her survival, a story that was yet to be concluded.

The next morning, Avni reached the hospital a little earlier than usual to give last touches to her presentation. It was one of those chilly winter mornings in Delhi. Her fur coat, a gift from her parents upon completing her graduation, gave her a much-needed warmth. *I wish we shared the same warmth in life as well.* She missed them every day. It was almost 8 a.m. by the time she finished giving final touches to her presentation. Everyone started trickling in slowly.

Soon, Dr Kapoor arrived and signalled her to start. She began the PowerPoint presentation. Her voice trembled a bit in the beginning, but Avni kept on going, slide after slide, and slowly regained her composure. She presented comprehensive details of about fifteen patients with HIV/AIDS. It felt good that no one was interrupting her during her talk. Avni always preferred the questioning to be reserved for the end. This was until she heard, "Excuse me!" She stopped speaking and looked up. He was sitting in the second row. She glanced over in his direction.

"I want to know about patient number twelve. What is your diagnosis?" Aakash asked.

"He has been admitted recently, just two days back. The patient has a history of prolonged fever, weight loss, liver and spleen enlargement and lymphadenopathy. The presumptive diagnosis is Tuberculosis. But investigations are being carried out for the final diagnosis," she replied.

"Have you taken his treatment history?" he asked, "And also the history about his occupation?"

"Actually, the patient is a little confused about his treatment history." And then, in an apologetic tone, she said, "I didn't ask about his occupation, I am sorry."

"Dr Avni, this is a government hospital. Patients who come here are not very educated. They won't tell you everything on their own. You have to seriously work upon them to elicit any worthwhile information," Aakash said with an obvious sarcasm in his voice. "You are not running a five-star clinic of your own where only rich, educated patients come for treatment."

For a moment, she thought he was again vindictive for reasons best known to him, but then strangely she instantly blocked out those thoughts and decided to focus on what he was saying. *Perhaps I have made a mistake.*

Before she could say anything in her defense, he spoke again, "This patient is a construction worker and at high risk of histoplasmosis because of his exposure to contaminated soil, bird manure and/or bat droppings."

She kept looking at him; not as an adversary, but as someone she admired for his sharp clinical sense. He was her senior, posted in the same unit; she remembered how keen she was to discuss her presentation with him, but was hesitant to do so.

He continued with his gaze firmly fixed on Avni, "The patient had already received antituberculosis treatment, but he didn't respond to it." He then looked around the room and then looked at her again before delivering the final onslaught, "One has to be careful to extract all details from the patient, which obviously you haven't."

I wish we had had this discussion before the formal presentation. Avni thought to herself.

"I am sorry for this lapse," she said, trying to keep her voice stable. "I'll be more careful in future."

Avni completed her remaining presentation without any further interference, but her outward calm was a mere facade in direct contrast to the disquiet she was feeling inside.

Avni had just concluded her presentation when she heard Dr Kapoor. He was speaking to Dr Pandey about her work. She looked up.

"Aakash has a lot of experience working with HIV/AIDS patients," Dr Kapoor said, "And since you are too busy with administrative responsibilities besides the academics, it's a good idea to have him on board. He can be of great help." Dr Kapoor added, "Avni can directly work with Aakash for her dissertation work."

Avni stood motionless, it was like a bolt from the blue. *How on earth was she expected to traverse the chasm between them!* Inadvertently, her eyes once again sought for any echo, any reaction from Aakash, but he looked as distant as ever.

"I think having him in the panel would certainly benefit her. She is sincere in her work, and Dr Aakash's help could make a huge difference in her dissertation work," Dr Pandey agreed instantly, but he seemed to know better, "We must ask if they are okay with it. There's no point imposing our will on them if they are not keen to work together."

Avni found herself baffled by this sudden development. After a long struggle, she had reached a stage in her life when she was looking forward to some serenity. Those years of pain were slowly fading in the hope of a new future. And now this uninvited guest was inevitably going to make her life difficult. It was not that she feared work, she was as committed to patients as he was, if not more. What she worried was his arrogance, his indifference. *How on earth was she going to work with such an insensitive person*? She had dealt with one in the past, and she did not want to go through it again. She was still lost in her thoughts when Dr Kapoor turned to ask, "Dr Avni, is this okay with you?"

No, it's not okay with me. She wanted to scream.

"Yes sir," she said meekly. *Not like I have a choice.*

Moments later, she heard Dr Kapoor asking the same question to Aakash, "Actually, I should have asked you first, but I am sure that you won't refuse. I know, you enjoy working with these patients." He smiled. "I guess it should be okay with you."

Aakash kept looking at Dr Kapoor for some time. His calm expression was not difficult to decipher. He was just not interested.

"Sir, I don't need to be involved with her work. I can always help her without being a part of the study," he finally uttered.

"Well, we want your full commitment, and that's only possible if you are officially involved with this work," Dr Pandey remarked.

"Probably..." Aakash was outwitted. He glanced at Avni who was looking down. "Okay sir, as you wish."

8

"Oh my god! I can't believe it. You are finally here." Avni jumped with joy when she saw her sister Sia at the airport. Sia had an official engagement in Delhi. She took this godsent opportunity to visit Avni. She was visiting her sister for the first time since she had moved here. They hugged with tears streaming down their faces. It had only been three months, but it seemed they were meeting after ages. Although Sia was not physically present with Avni, she was an unseen force behind her sister's efforts to get over her past. She was the one who kept telling her to not look at the future with the prism of the past. While Avni used to be volatile, impulsive and short-tempered, Sia, although younger, was mature, relaxed and calm. Of course, all that had changed for Avni now. Life had taught her the lessons that she couldn't inherit by default from her mother. She had been more like her father. Honest, forthright, but very aggressive. Perhaps time was the best teacher.

"I missed you so much!" Sia kissed her. "How is my little prince? You know what, I miss him more than I miss you."

With her parents not so warm towards little Vivan, Avni cherished Sia's unconditional love for her nephew.

"I bet you do." Avni laughed. Both sisters then walked briskly out of the airport terminal.

Sia jumped in the passenger seat. "What a beautiful car, I am so proud of you."

"Yes, one luxury that I gifted myself after coming here!" Avni took a deep breath.

Sia knew what was hidden in that sigh... *all that was lost, all that could have been.*

"You have done a great job!"

Avni glanced at her, momentarily taking her eyes off the road and smiled. "You are my biggest cheerleader."

"I am serious." Sia touched her elbow.

"I am also serious. I wouldn't have survived without you. Even Ma couldn't forgive me for creating havoc in our small, beautiful family... but you did!"

"Now stop feeling guilty. You can't do that to yourself for the rest of your life." Sia diverted the discussion, "Tell me about my sweetheart. How is Vivan?"

Avni's eyes lit up with the mere mention of his name. Her sadness suddenly disappeared and she smiled broadly.

"He has started to recognize everyone now." Her voice had so much excitement. "He's fine with Mrs Joseph during the day, but by six in the evening, he starts looking for me." Avni gestured towards her mobile phone. "Look at his photos."

When they reached home, Sia immediately went to cuddle her nephew. Vivan recognized her instantly and cooed happily.

"It looks like he is enjoying the change. He gets fed up with seeing only his mother and me all the time," Mrs Joseph commented. All of them laughed.

Sia then took out a bag full of gifts for Vivan. "Mum has sent this for him." She looked at Avni. "You know they went shopping as soon as they got to know about my trip."

"They..." She looked at her sister in utter disbelief with wide eyes. "You mean Daddy too?"

"That's right. I think he couldn't take it at the time. His favourite child. His replica. Not doing what he always wanted her to do." She paused, smiled and then looked at Avni, "You were always the bright one. I was the average types."

"Now stop it. You are doing so well as a financial analyst at a business firm," Avni said.

"But the facts remain that you cracked medicine entrance test. You were like a dream come true for our father. A star in the family," she said, her eyes getting moist. "Perhaps he never shows it, but he couldn't let go of you, however much he pretended." She knew that Daddy missed Avni severely, but out of his characteristic stubbornness, couldn't reach out to her. Their mother had taken everything in a better way. She was a practical woman who would go with the flow of life. Although Avni didn't share the same closeness with her mother, she tactically supported her from a distance. Avni remembered how all hell broke loose when she returned to them with a month old Vivan and announced her separation from Samir. She never got married as per their wishes and now was back, that too with a child. Her father didn't want her to stay at their home. And the stubborn daughter that she was, she didn't beg. She remained in the married accommodation hostel of Allahabad Medical School and Hospitals for three months before moving to Delhi. Her friend Anita had lent her a room for the time being. Her mother's invisible help was in the form of Mrs Joseph who she desperately hired to look after Vivan.

Tears started flowing from Avni's eyes. "But he was so angry just a few months back when my divorce was being finalized."

"He was. But since the time you have cleared your post-graduatc entrance exam and moved here, things started changing."

"But he didn't even bother to have a glimpse of Vivan when he was born."

"Time heals everything!" Sia hugged her. "It's all going to be okay."

"I feel so much better today. All along, besides meeting my regrets every day, I was living with the guilt that I have wronged them." The white of Avni's eyes had turned dark pink as she mouthed those words. Sia looked at her sister, wondering why she had to suffer so much.

"In fact, I overheard them the other day, talking about getting you a place to stay here. I mean a good one," she said. "I had told mum earlier that you are renting a two-bedroom flat and that too in a not-so-great suburb."

She looked at Sia, her eyes conveying what she was feeling inside. "Sia, parents do so much for their children. But we never really understand them. I always felt they were my enemy when I was seeing Samir."

""Now stop being negative," Sia said.

"Okay, okay. Should I call Dad?" Avni asked.

"I don't think so. Wait a little more. Let him feel completely comfortable, ready enough for you and Vivan. Give him some time, ad everything will be back to normal."

Both sisters then opened the gifts. There were clothes and toys, and also a beautiful card for Vivan, signed off with 'Love and hugs, Nana and Nani.' Avni kissed the card. "This one is the most precious gift."

It was already five in the evening when both sisters finished their first round of long-awaited heart to heart chat. "I am hungry!" Sia said.

"Oh, I am so sorry darling!" Avni squealed. "Let me fix dinner for you."

Sia cradled Vivan in her arms and played with him while Avni and Mrs Joseph prepared dinner.

After dinner, Avni tucked Vivan into bed. Then, both sisters sat in the living room again for the next round of chat. They had to compensate for a lot of lost time. And every minute was precious since Sia had to catch a flight back home to Allahabad the next day, right after her meeting at the company's headquarters. There was so much to catch up on, so much to share.

"Tell me what's happening in your life?" Avni coaxed Sia. "Have you found your Mr Right?"

"Not yet. You will be the first to know!" Sia winked at her. They laughed. "Sometimes I want to leave it to Dad. Want to give him the satisfaction of finding a match for me."

"You mean you wouldn't mind an arranged marriage?" Avni looked surprised.

"No harm. What difference does it make?"

"A lot of difference! Like, don't you want to get to know the person before marrying him?"

"I don't know if that makes any difference," Sia said reflectively. She didn't want to state the obvious.

The meaning of her words didn't go unnoticed by her sister. They understood each other so well. Nothing could remain hidden between the two.

"You are right Sia." Avni sipped her jasmine tea. "Perhaps you can never actually know a person. There are so many layers to someone's personality, and you can only get to know them one by one." There were many things she found out about Samir after their marriage. Every day, a new layer of his personality was revealed, unseen and unheard of before.

"We can't actually generalize, sometimes it works, but it's all destined," Sia tactically retracted her own statement, not wanting to hurt her sister.

"Hmm..." Avni had learnt her lesson the hard way.

After a moment of pause, Avni looked at her sister. "So coming back to layers of personality, I have seen a classic example at my medical school."

"And what's that?" Sia was curious, happy that they were digressing from painful, senseless issues about Avni's past.

"This one is a senior registrar at my department. He has something against me, picks on me every time I work with him."

"But why?" Sia seemed genuinely perplexed, knowing that her sister had just joined the new place, "Especially with you, such a pretty doctor! Well anyway, you haven't been here long enough to be able to offend anyone!"

"Come on... leave that pretty thing out, no one cares." Avni mocked. "But whenever we work together, I tend to screw something up, but even if I don't, he alleges that I have."

"What? This is insane."

"It's funny." She paused. "No, actually it's not. I feel scared of working with him." Avni looked serious. "He reminds me of Samir sometimes. How he used to make me feel, 'good for nothing' sorts."

"Are you sure?" Sia felt terrible that her sister was facing the same pain that she was running away from.

"At least, this is what it looks like. But apparently, Aakash is a very driven sort of person, giving hundred percent to whatever he does. Perhaps that's why he's so hard on me because he wants the best for his patients." Her eyes looked as innocent as ever, Sia thought.

"Perhaps!" Sia gave her sister a meaningful look. "Be careful. You are a little weak when it comes to reading people."

"Yes, you know it!"

"Let me see what he looks like." Sia felt a little perplexed by the mixed feelings that Avni had for this man, hate but sort of admiration for his professional acumen.

"What's the name?" Sia was now in complete spying mood.

"Aakash Mehta," Avni said.

Sia instantly looked him up on Google, and he was apparently all over it. Within seconds, they could browse through his personal and professional profiles. Sia suddenly found herself staring at his profile picture. "Oh my god, he is so handsome!"

"He is pretty popular with the ladies!" Avni said after a fleeting glance at the picture.

"Isn't it all a little confusing? His profile doesn't really match his attitude," Sia said as she turned the laptop off. She knew that she was interrogating Avni so much because she cared for her. Sia had seen Avni being reduced to nothing from her glorious days, just because of that one mistake of marrying Samir Verma. She didn't want her sister to go through anything of that sort again. And from what Avni had told her about him, he looked like a clone of Samir, handsome, but with an uncaring heart.

"It is confusing, but why should we care!" Avni looked distant. "I have nothing to do with him, except for his guidance for my dissertation work that was kind of imposed on me."

"You could have always refused to work under him." Sia was at her usual best. Sensible and pragmatic.

"I don't think that would have been feasible, especially knowing his expertise in HIV/AIDS," Avni said.

"It'll be alright, don't worry." Sia smiled.

9

Aakash was in his cubicle after finishing the morning OPD. As usual, he was checking his emails before going for lunch when he heard someone knocking at the door. It wasn't an easy decision for Avni. She contemplated at least a thousand times before approaching him for this particular patient, one of her dissertation cases.

After the dissertation's progress report presentation, it was clear to her that she couldn't avoid him. Still, there was no way Avni could have understood why he was the way he was. It was incomprehensible. A man who had everything in the world he could ask for, and yet, so unhappy. Today, once again, it took all her determination to see him.

"Yes. Come in." His deep voice reverberated in the corridor.

She slowly opened the door to find him working on his computer, so engrossed that he didn't even bother to look up at the intruder.

Avni waited for a few seconds, but after not getting any response, called out, "Dr Aakash!"

That was a familiar voice, a voice that had intrigued him since the day he had seen her first. He raised his head to find her standing at the door. She looked so beautiful in a printed white churidar kurta reflecting the myriad hues of spring. The curls of her auburn hair fell on her shoulders. For a moment, he couldn't move his gaze away from her. But the very next moment, he was his usual self, unconcerned and distant. It was as if he didn't want to acknowledge his own feelings with the belief that they would die a natural death if they remain unacknowledged. And it worked.

"Yes, Dr Avni." He closed his laptop and gestured her to sit.

With hesitant steps, Avni moved forward and sat facing him directly. However much she tried to pretend otherwise, she felt uncomfortable, and it didn't go unnoticed by Aakash who was incidentally on the same boat.

"I wanted to talk about a newly married couple, Mr and Mrs Chandra whom you saw in your last OPD," she said.

"Hmm..." He looked uninterested. "What's there to discuss?"

"Mr Chandra is living with HIV while Mrs Chandra is negative for the virus. And you might be aware that they want to have a baby."

"Yes, I am aware." He raised his eyebrows as if finding the discussion completely irrelevant.

"I understand that you are not in favour of the pregnancy," she said without getting flustered.

"Yes, I am not," he said. "There is nothing to discuss in this case, Dr Avni!"

"It would have been okay if the wife didn't want to carry the baby. But she really wants to," she said.

"Dr Avni! He exclaimed, "Excuse me!" The sarcasm in his voice didn't go unnoticed by Avni. But she didn't flinch. She'd had two years to get good at it. She felt herself becoming very still. "The patient has HIV. He could always pass on the virus to his wife and child."

She calmly replied, "Luckily, we do have antiretroviral drugs for taking care of the situation. As we know, children born to even HIV positive mother can escape HIV if the mother is on antiretroviral drugs." She paused looking somewhere in the distance, as if thinking about something before adding, "Not everyone is so fortunate in love. To have someone who is even willing to risk her life for their dream is exceptional." Though she regretted the spontaneous verbalization of her thoughts a moment later, it certainly left Aakash wondering if that kind of love ever exists. He had never thought of love in this perspective. For him, love was perhaps nothing more than a momentary liking, an ephemeral phase. And after that moment was over, if you are still together, it was more like a cohabitation. Something just like his parents had where by default, the so-called love withers away, slowly, in diminishing doses and what remains is a perpetual sense of profound emptiness that could never be fulfilled by anything that world has to offer.

"You are right Dr Avni, we do have antiretroviral treatment available for the patients, and they can always choose to have a baby." Strangely, Aakash found himself agreeing to her. He couldn't say that it was the first time in life that someone had made him realize about the highest potential of love, that to love someone means to care for the other's happiness more than yours, even if it meant to make difficult choices. Choices that could be both painful and regrettable.

Vivan was almost nine months old now. He had started crawling all over the place at home. Avni had to re-organize her small home to meet his needs. He was a hyperactive baby, keeping Mrs Joseph on her toes throughout the day. Avni was paranoid about Vivan playing with the power-points and had secured them all with duct-tapes. She called in a carpenter to smoothen and round off the sharp edges of the central table in the lounge to prevent any injury to Vivan as he frequently used the table as a support to stand. Avni could never get over the twinkle in his eyes when he would be successful in his attempt to stand up. The pleasure of watching him learning to live life, one step at a time, was incomparable to anything in the world, she thought.

Her worry started when the new duty roster was released. She would have to be on call one night every week. Earlier, it used to be an emergency call once a month, and she would manage things at home with Mrs Joseph. There was also a medical camp that was being organized in Faridabad, a satellite town near Delhi, in a few months' time and her name was in the list of doctors who were supposed to attend. *How good would it have been if I did my residency from Allahabad? At least, Sia would have been able to come over to stay with Vivan at night. Her work wouldn't have entailed night shifts, and she would have been more than happy to help.*

Suddenly she wanted to call her mother and ask her for help. She thought of asking her to stay with her until Vivan was more stable. Her father was still working, but he was quite capable of taking care of himself. Moreover, they had an army of servants to help them, thanks to his high position in the government. But then she decided against it. After her marriage and painful divorce, her mother had maintained a grudging distance from her. Avni could understand now, after giving birth to Vivan, how much a parent loves their child. She didn't realize all this when she had decided to elope with Samir, leaving her parents with shock and grief.

Avni decided to talk to Dr Neha Tripathi about her dilemma of leaving Vivan during the on-call nights. Being a senior and a well-meaning person, she might have a good advice for her, she thought. She messaged her, and Neha updated her that she was out of town, but would love to see her next week when she was back.

❖

As soon as she finished seeing her last patient in the morning round, she saw Nikhil and Sandeep waving at her from the other end of the corridor. She stopped and waited for them as they walked towards her.

"Let's have coffee." Nikhil chirped. She could sense the admiring looks both men seemed to be giving her and pretended not to notice. She remembered how Samir made her feel when she would dress up after they got married, sometimes just for him, hoping he would compliment her. But he would only be plain indifferent, pretending she didn't exist. It was like *she was never good enough for him. Never.* She shuddered at the memory.

The three of them walked together to the small café near the hospital.

"Well Avni, how's life treating you?" Nikhil started the conversation as soon as they were seated.

"Not bad! I am surviving. What about you?" She smiled, giving proof that she had indeed survived the past. Nikhil liked that now she was not so reserved. The degree of her aloofness had receded a bit.

"Oh, I love it. After managing to enter into such a coveted residency program, now I am enjoying life to the fullest. After hospital hours, it's mostly movies, clubs and pubs. Life can't be better." His eyes gleamed with happiness. "Hostel life is bliss. No responsibilities. No dictates of parents."

"What about your relationship status?" Sandeep winked as he asked Nikhil.

Avni was silently enjoying their conversation. She had never experienced this kind of light exchanges. Before she realized, Avni was married to Samir, the first boy she met when she had just started her internship. He was her boyfriend for a couple of months and then it was marriage followed by a divorce; all in quick succession, like a lightning strike that illuminated the sky and then destroys the area where it strikes.

"Well, I am still single." Nikhil's eyes travelled to Avni who pretended to be oblivious to his cue. The corners of her mouth curled a bit upwards as if to show that although she was enjoying the exchanges, she was not into it.

Coffee arrived, and they went on to talk about hospital stuff.

"Thank god you were proven right in Mr Singh's case, Avni. I am sure Dr Aakash would have been happy if you weren't." Sandeep then looked around and then whispered, "What a little monster he is. Keeps working like crazy and also expects everyone to follow his madness."

Avni just smiled. She had no intention of entering into any controversy and that too with that impossibly arrogant man who was now also her co-supervisor in the thesis.

"I have a strong hunch, though." Nikhil glanced at Avni. "I think Dr Aakash has a special affinity for Avni!"

Although he was trying to say it humorously, Sandeep could feel a tinge of pain in Nikhil's voice along with the fear of losing out to Aakash in some invisible, perceived competition in wooing Avni.

"Are you crazy?" Avni couldn't stop herself now. "He hates me like anything. Who does that to a new resident on her first emergency call?" She continued, "And he didn't stop at that. He picks on me as soon as he gets an opportunity." For the first time since joining, she found herself blurting out how she felt, sharing her dilemma with people she hardly knew.

"I reckon he likes you."

Avni was taken aback, but she said in a cold voice, "I am a married woman, with a child."

Avni's eyes couldn't miss the perplexed look that instantly descended on Nikhil's face. It was a mixture of awe and shock. She didn't tell them that she was single now, a divorcee and had decided to remain single all her life for she could not afford to be hurt again in love.

10

Aakash was at a school friend's birthday party. Rajiv Mehra had inherited his father's business and was now working hard to take it to newer heights. Married to Ria, a girl he met in school, Rajiv lived at one of the prominent postcodes of Delhi surrounded by neatly manicured green lawns and majestic fountains. With waiters eager to serve the most expensive delicacies accompanied with alcohol from around the world, the party was getting heady with the scent of expensive perfume worn by the guests, all too obvious signs of his high status in the society.

Aakash looked handsome, as always. He looked like an enigma, making one want to know the deep secrets of his heart, to understand and love him. Incidentally, that someone was also present at this party. The beautiful Priya, Rajiv's younger sister.

Priya had inherited the best features from her parents. She looked stunning with her flawless complexion and beautiful looks. She knew Aakash since the time he was in school with her brother. He used to regularly come over to hang out with him. She remembered how she always wanted to join them, but was almost always rebuffed. From PlayStation, X-box, Nintendo to cricket and football, they played everything. She was envious of their friendship as she didn't have any such close friend. So much time had passed. Both the boys had chosen different career paths and slowly drifted apart because of their busy lives. Priya had just completed her degree in English literature from the prestigious Delhi University and was now planning to pursue her Master's from London. Aakash's mother, Dr Rita Mehta absolutely loved Priya. She was like the daughter she never had. Priya would always drop in at their home to see his mother, and she always made time for her. They would spend time in the kitchen, exchanging exotic recipes and baking ideas.

Aakash did not have much to do with her except make small talk here and there, but it warmed his heart to see Priya spending time with his mother. He knew how lonely his mother used to get at home. It was alright when she was busy at her clinic, but at home, she didn't have the companionship with her husband of twenty years that one would expect. His father, the great Dr R.K. Mehta, had a love marriage, something that was not very common in India at that time. But over the years, they drifted apart, slowly, in fleeting doses; the mask came off, and their raw, opposite natures couldn't survive the assault of time. They remained together, helplessly denying their colossal mismatch to themselves, not opting for divorce, perhaps for the sake of Aakash, but their home indeed lost its warmth over the time.

The cold vibes had enveloped Aakash in their grip, even when he was very young to understand all the complicated dynamics of human relationships. The emptiness that he felt from those times still haunted him today. He tried everything possible to get rid of the void that he felt deep inside his heart – keeping himself busy with studies, sports, and dating girls now and then, but somehow nothing could fill the ever-persisting vacuum in the deepest recesses of his heart.

His mother wanted him to get married to Priya. She thought that she was the only person who could really understand him and make him happy. Aakash wanted to make his mother happy, but he was not sure if he would be a happy man after marrying Priya. Priya, on the other hand, had no doubts. She liked him so much. Since she was very young, since the days he used to visit their home to play with Rajiv. He was the one her dreams were made of.

Priya's eyes were searching for that one person today as well. Once she found out that he was coming, she had taken great care in getting ready for the party. Her sister-in-law, Ria had teased her. "So, Aakash is coming today! I guess that's the reason for you looking so gorgeous tonight." She blushed. How much she pined for him, waiting for him to tell her that he loved her just as much.

Suddenly the man she was pining for, appeared in front of her. Her Aakash. For a moment, she was speechless. Thanks to Rajiv, who somehow instantly appeared on the scene and started off a conversation to make things smoother for her. "Priya is planning to go to London for her Master's."

"I see," Aakash spoke as he swirled his glass of wine. Her heart sank on seeing his ambiguous response, with no change in his demeanor. "So, when you are starting the course?"

"I'm heading there this July," she said. "It's a two-year course, starts in September." She wanted him to say that she shouldn't go so early, or better, she shouldn't go at all.

"Okay!" His eyes met hers. "We will miss you."

She smiled, so happy to listen to those words that kept the flame of hope alive in her heart. At least now she had something to hold on to. Perhaps, he isn't so expressive, she justified. *Sublime, how in love, you find little things to keep you going and not let you give up.*

"We sure, will." Rajiv put his arms over her shoulder, affectionately pulling her closer. "My darling little sister!"

"So, soon, you'll be a famous novelist," Aakash commented.

Rajiv laughed. "Yes, my dear sister will be a great, world-renowned novelist."

Who wants to be famous? I just want you, damn it. Don't you get it? I won't go if you stop me. Priya wanted to shout, but she just smiled again.

Slowly, the party gathered momentum. The crowd increased, and so did the volume of the music. Aakash was being coaxed by his friends to sing, but he was a few drinks down, too drunk to sing coherently. After staying a while, Aakash decided to leave. His head felt heavy under the effect of alcohol. He just wanted to be alone. Rajiv instructed his driver to drop him home.

After finishing up at the OPD, Avni was waiting for Dr Neha in the hospital cafeteria. She had just been waiting a few minutes when she saw Neha walking towards her. They exchanged smiles.

"So how are you settling in?" Dr Neha was her usual spirited self. "I hope Unit II is treating you well."

"I'm good." There was something about her that made Avni comfortable in her presence from day one. "I wish you could have continued in Unit II," she said.

Neha smiled. "Don't worry. You'll be fine with Dr Aakash."

"He is a difficult man, hard to manage and impossible to please." Avni rolled her eyes. "I'll need some advice from you."

"Any day, any time." Dr Neha opened her lunch box. "Can we have our lunch as well as we talk? I am starving."

"Of course," Avni picked the spoon. "The duty roster is out. As expected, I am on-call on certain nights as well."

"That's normal, nothing unusual." Dr Neha took a bite.

"I know. But Dr Aakash seems to be too strict about the duties." Dr Neha could see fear mixed with anxiety in her eyes.

"It's okay. You are a very sincere registrar. What's there to worry about?" She was genuinely surprised.

"If there is an emergency at home, I am not sure he will allow me to swap my shift with someone else," she said.

"That shouldn't be a problem. It happens to everyone, so it'll be alright to swap things around." She was a little puzzled as to why Avni was worrying about routine adjustments.

"The thing is, I have a small child at home." Avni avoided Dr Neha's eyes as she spoke those words.

Neha looked at her as if she had just dropped a bomb.

After a long pause where she kept stirring her coffee, she said, "So you are married, and that too with a kid. That's a surprise."

"Well, I am a single mother." She looked at her and then looked away. "A divorcee."

For a moment, Dr Neha didn't know what to say. But then she recovered, "I understand, it must be hard."

"I live with my son and my housekeeper, Mrs Joseph." Avni said, "That's okay. But sometimes, nights can be difficult with a nine-month-old child."

"It must be." Neha finished her coffee that they had ordered after having their lunch. "How about your parents?"

"They live in Allahabad." Avni sipped her coffee. It was cold, but she kept on drinking. How much she would have liked to avoid all this conversation, anything that reminded her of her past. She didn't tell Neha that her parents were unhappy with her and she couldn't expect any help from them, at least not for now. If not for Aakash's abstruse nature, she would not have had to discuss all this with Neha, who was still a stranger to her, however nice she was. She detested seeking sympathy from anyone on account of her life's dilemmas.

"Okay, now don't worry so much!" Dr Neha's warmth put Avni in a better frame of mind. The awkwardness she felt while discussing her personal life diluted a bit. "It's not an unusual situation. Anyone can be in your position." She paused for a few seconds and then looked at Avni with her eyebrows raised, "Aakash can be difficult sometimes. Generally, we try not to involve the faculty and manage these things between ourselves. But he has his own idiosyncrasies."

"Exactly, that's the thing that worries me sometimes." Avni promptly added. "I wonder why he is like that, although I do feel that he doesn't mean any harm."

"Yes, that's the way Aakash is." Neha took a deep breath. "He was my classmate. We did MBBS and then post-graduation together. He has changed over the years. He has changed a lot."

"Oh really, your classmate?" exclaimed Avni, not being able to imagine Aakash as a regular kid who studied with Neha.

"I hate saying this, but I wonder if it's anything to do with his father's nature," Neha remarked. Avni remembered the conversation she had with the emergency nurse on her first day, about his father's rigorous nature.

Dr Neha continued, "Although his father is excellent professionally, he is a tough person with an overtly dominating attitude. Perhaps the situation is the same at home. The rumour has it that he doesn't have a cordial relationship with his wife. I am sure Aakash must have been affected by all this."

"I understand," Avni said, clearly seeing how Neha reluctantly told her everything. She didn't seem like a person who enjoyed discussing anyone's personal life.

"But you should not worry. Aakash is a good person. I think he will understand your problems if you are honest with him," Neha said.

Avni wondered how she could be honest with a person who didn't even want to communicate properly, but she didn't say anything. She faintly smiled.

On the way back home, Avni thought about what Dr Neha told her. *Was his arrogance a way to avoid entering into any delicate situation? Wasn't she the same with her aloofness, a strategy to prevent any future grief? Didn't she change because of what Samir did to her? Perhaps, for him, it was all about forgetting himself, and for her, it was all about finding herself. He seemed to be trying to resist the pain while she had slowly learned that for healing to occur, she had to feel the pain, to see what it's trying to teach her.* After this conversation with Dr Neha, things hadn't changed much for Avni as far as her worries were concerned, but at least her dislike for him lessened a bit.

The dreaded M&M conference, dubbed as firing squad by the registrars, was being held as per the schedule on Wednesday morning. Avni was sitting with other junior registrars at the back. Compared to the horror of the first day as a registrar posted in an emergency, today was a relaxed day. She was more of a spectator than a participant. She liked it this way, hidden, unnoticed, lost in the crowd, while having an ordinary existence.

The senior registrars from both units, Dr Prakash from Unit I and Dr Shiv Mathur, a new senior registrar who had recently joined Unit II were presenting their cases as per the protocol. Avni was a little scared when she had to work with Dr Shiv, probably because of her unpleasant experience while working with Aakash for the first time. Shiv was a tall, thin man with expressive eyes. His bespectacled face made him look a little serious, but that was effectively neutralized by his charming dimpled smile and infectious enthusiasm. For Avni, working with him was entirely opposite to working with Aakash. *He made you so comfortable that you forgot that you were working with a senior.* In no time, Avni felt at ease with him. The emergency duty with him was like any other ordinary day, uneventful.

After Dr Prakash finished the presentation from Unit I, Dr Shiv got up and walked up to the podium to discuss his presentation from Unit II. He crisply summed up all the cases. There was nothing unusual; no unexplained morbidity or mortality. He had almost finished the presentation when he seemed to remember something.

"Ah, I forgot to tell you something important that happened during an emergency." He paused, and his eyes searched for Avni. He looked at her and then continued, "I take sole responsibility for the mistake. It could have been a disaster but for Dr Avni's quick presence of mind and action."

Avni could feel herself blushing. She was not used to someone praising her publicly and especially at this forum where she had been blamed for her delayed actions not long ago.

"There was one patient, Mr Ravi, a 50-year-old man who had come to emergency complaining of heartburn and indigestion. I advised him that it must be gastritis and prescribed him an antacid." He threw another quick glance at Avni, "But Dr Avni, who had also happened to see the patient, thought otherwise. She instantly sent the patient for an ECG and rightly so, as it turned out to be a heart attack. Thankfully, he was diagnosed well in time and could be saved. All the credit goes to Dr Avni."

Dr Kapoor and Dr Pandey almost simultaneously turned back to look for Avni amongst the crowd of scrubs. She could feel admiring eyes on her from almost everyone present there. Avni used to get uncomfortable at such collective applause, but today it felt good, like a redemption. Her past reputation of being a careless person suddenly seemed to fade away. She knew she was not extraordinary, but Avni also knew that she was not an irresponsible person as had been made out by Aakash. He was noticeably the only one who seemed to remain unmoved. But no one knew what he was feeling inside, a tinge of jealousy for Dr Shiv Mathur, something that he had never felt for anybody before. He couldn't figure it out initially – *was he feeling this way because he was proven wrong regarding Avni's competence or was it because of Shiv praising her? Why should he be jealous if someone was praising her? Why was he feeling something that he had never felt before?* It was the first time in his life that something had kept bothering him, long after the meeting had finished.

11

A medical camp was organized by the Delhi Medical School and Hospitals in a nearby suburban town.. The name of the team that was going this year was announced. Avni had no idea about it as it was only announced a day before, when she was on leave looking for a new house. The house hunting was prompted after Sia's visit, who had indicated that her parents were willing to support her financially. She had gone to inspect a property with Sia, who was, as usual, paying a flying visit to her sister. The small house where she was staying was not ideal for a toddler. The neighborhood where they lived was not what she preferred either. The streets were quite narrow, there were no parks around and there were a few safety concerns as well. Their mother was getting paranoid about them, and her father had asked Sia to quickly help Avni in moving to a better place. Sia, the bridge between her parents and sister, was doing her best.

When Avni reached the department in the morning, she glanced at the notice board while crossing the office of the HOD. "Faridabad Medical Camp", it was written. She decided to check if her name also figured in the list of doctors who were supposed to attend the two-day camp. As it was, she was endlessly worried about leaving Vivan in case her name was on the list. He was now relatively settled with her once a fortnight emergency night duty, but she was not sure about being away from him for at least seventy-two hours and that too far away from Delhi.

Her fears came true. She saw her name. Besides her Dr Aakash, Dr Nikhil, Dr Sandeep, and a new house officer, Dr Rekha Agarwal were going. The camp was organized to monitor the lifestyle diseases in the neighboring population, their timely prevention and cure. No matter how much she disliked it, there was no way she was going to get out of this. It was mandatory. At most, she could request to postpone it for some time, but she was not sure how she would be placed in future. It was best to be done with it.

Moreover, she was in no mood to plead with the camp's chief in-charge, Dr Aakash. As she walked towards the wards, she could feel a knot in her stomach. She again thought that she had made a mistake by opting for a different city to do her residency. Sia would have definitely helped had she stayed in Allahabad. A million thoughts were crossing her mind when she saw Aakash enter the ward. He was walking towards the nurses' station. She had just started seeing her first patient. She stole a glance at him as she flipped through the patient's report. He was talking to the duty nurse. For a moment, her dilemma, the anxiety that she was feeling, tried to take over her rational thinking. She wanted to go up to him and ask him if any alternate arrangement could be made. But then the other part of her brain advised her against it. There's no point being honest with him. He wouldn't understand.

She saw him walking towards her as she finished up with the patient.

"Hi, Dr Avni!" He seemed to be in a better mood than usual. He smelled so fresh. Summer had started, and it reflected in his immaculate dressing style, a white linen shirt with folded sleeves and beige cotton trousers. *Perhaps, he is not taking rounds today. He was not wearing the doctor's coat.*

"Hello, Dr Aakash!" She looked into his eyes. He looked back, and their eyes remain locked for a moment.

"Did you see the list? Your name is amongst the registrars who are heading to the medical camp."

"Yes, I did. It'll be a good experience, I reckon," she lied. She couldn't bring herself to tell him what she was actually feeling. Her pragmatic reply concealed her emotions effectively.

"Great! All of you, the registrars, house officer, intern, nurses and other paramedics will travel by the bus arranged by the department in the morning. I will join you guys later in the day." He waited for a moment as if expecting any question from her about the camp. She didn't ask.

"I'll drive there on my own," he said.

Why is he telling me this? Possibly to show that he is too important to travel on the bus with us, she wondered.

In the evening, she reluctantly made all the preparations for camp. She looked at her son. He was playfully hovering around the living room, trying to stand with the support of the table, unaware of the dilemma that his mother was going through. He lifted his chin. His twinkling eyes and innocent smile simply melted her heart. *You are my world.* She took him in her arms and hugged him tightly. Suddenly all those years of pain that she had endured with Samir seemed worthwhile. Even if she had lost all in that relationship, she had gained Vivan, her most treasured possession. *It helped that Samir never asked for his custody. How could she have survived without Vivan?* Avni had to leave home by 6 a.m. to catch the bus. Vivan was still sleeping. She tiptoed into his room and gently kissed him, trying not to wake him up. It would be too hard to leave if he did. Mrs Joseph came to see her off. She gave her some instructions regarding Vivan to which, Mrs Joseph smiled back in response. Avni turned the keys into the ignition and waved her goodbye before she drove off to the hospital.

The bus reached Faridabad at around 8 a.m. All team members checked into their hotel before walking down to the campsite, a peripheral health centre. The medical camp had been well advertised by the hospital authorities. There was a long list of patients waiting to attend the camp. Aakash was already there. He was giving instructions to the local staff who worked at the centre. He hardly noticed when his team arrived. He was checking the blood pressure equipment when Nikhil announced their arrival, "Sir, we are here!"

Aakash turned to look at them. "Welcome! How was your trip?" For the first time since Avni had known him, he was looking a bit relaxed. Maybe it was the fact that he was working away from the hospital campus or it was something else, she couldn't decide. *It's going to make everyone's job less stressful.*

"Great! An early morning ride is always good. Less traffic."

"Okay then, let's begin. Hope you all had some breakfast!"

"Actually we haven't," Avni heard herself say. She was quite hungry. She left home in a hurry, not thinking about food.

To her relief, she heard others joining in, "We didn't have time in the morning!"

Aakash raised his eyes and looked at her. She was wearing blue jeans with a black top. Her peachy crème complexion seemed so fresh in the summer morning. He wondered what made her look so attractive ever since the first time he saw her. There was nothing particularly extraordinary about her, but she still looked so pretty.

To her surprise and to everybody else's as well, he didn't get irritated or upset. He half-smiled. "Okay, no problem. Let me ask the medical officer in-charge to arrange for breakfast here." He looked towards the adjoining room. "We do have a spare room for our staff."

They had a quick breakfast before they started working. Avni was pleasantly surprised to see plenty of patients travel from distant villages for the check-up. Under Dr Aakash's sharp eyes, the team continuously worked till late evening, barring a short lunch break. People who had significant health issues were referred to the hospital, and others were given treatment on site with a promise to be followed up at the next medical camp. It was heart-warming to see how grateful people were for their efforts. Some of them had even come with gifts, things that grew in their farms, fresh vegetables and milk. The satisfaction on their faces, the warmth and the gratitude in their eyes was worth all the effort. In moments like these, Aakash would feel proud of the profession he chose. It gave him some fulfillment and lessened that feeling of loneliness and emptiness he carried with him every day.

The plan for the evening was a mini-cultural get-together followed by dinner. Everyone was tired, so the idea was to unwind and have a little fun before the grueling schedule of the next day. Avni was happy that it was an impromptu, casual get together. There were no formalities, no dressing up needed. If she had her way, she would have attended it in her pajamas, she thought with a smile.

Nikhil and Sandeep had taken it upon themselves to organize the evening. It was a little surprise that Aakash had accepted the proposal without much fuss. At around 8 p.m., everyone assembled in the hotel's conference room. People were mingling, having a great time eating and drinking. Sandeep came up with the idea to have a musical competition. He suggested that they should split into two groups. Everyone promptly agreed, and the game began. Both teams positioned themselves opposite to each other. After ages, Aakash was enjoying it all. He had been to so many big parties with hundreds of guests playing games and singing, but until today, he had never felt the sheer pleasure of such simple moments. That's when he heard her laughter. With her head thrown back, Avni was laughing at some joke shared amongst the opposing group. He had never heard her laugh before. She always looked aloof or seemed to be engrossed in her work. The tinkling sound of her laughter strangely made him feel good. He didn't know the answer as to why he was feeling so, but it didn't matter. For the first time in his life, it was all about enjoying the moment rather than finding the reason for it.

It was now Aakash's turn to sing when his eyes again travelled to the spot where Avni was standing before. She wasn't there anymore. His eyes circled around the room, but he couldn't find her anywhere. He started singing, but his eyes didn't stop looking for her. Finally, she appeared, walking in with her mobile phone glued to her ear. She looked lost. *She must have gone outside because the reception seemed to be weak inside.* She had now lost all interest in the game and was just frantically calling or texting, walking in and out of the room.

It was almost 10 p.m. Aakash's team had won the game against Nikhil's team. Everyone headed towards the dining area. Avni followed them with slow steps, still busy with her phone.

"When are you going to eat?" Nikhil asked when she didn't pick up a dinner plate, "You are so glued to your phone."

"You go ahead, I'll join you soon." Avni looked hassled but didn't say much.

Later, Rekha handed over a plate with some food to her when she saw that she was still not eating. "All well?" she asked Avni.

"Just trying to settle a little issue at home," Avni replied absent-mindedly. "It should be okay."

Aakash's eyes would travel towards her every now and then. He felt that same tinge of jealousy that he had on the day Dr Shiv was praising her. *Why am I feeling this way? Why was he so concerned about what she was doing?*

The dinner was soon over. Avni had barely eaten anything from her plate. She was just picking on the food. Everyone started leaving the hall to retire to their rooms. It was going to be a long day tomorrow and a good night's sleep was undoubtedly needed. Avni also walked out with her room-mate Rekha.

It was after midnight when Aakash heard a knock on his door. He ignored it at first, being in a deep sleep, but the constant knocking forced him out of his slumber, and he answered. "Who is it?

"Sir, Sandeep here. We have a little emergency." Aakash opened the door. "Avni has to travel back to Delhi. Her son has some problem, it seems."

"Where is the bus driver?" he asked.

"He lives in a nearby suburb. He requested for leave tonight to meet his folks."

"Oh yes! I remember. Where is Dr Avni?"

"She is in her room."

A taxi wouldn't be a very safe option, Aakash found himself thinking. *But why am I so concerned. People travel at night all the time, including girls.* But a voice in his head was cautioning him to be careful and not let Avni travel alone.

As if on cue, Sandeep said, "You could drive her down."

"Ah, that's an option. Let me see." There was an unmistakable hesitation in his voice.

He walked with Sandeep to Avni's room. The door was ajar. Rekha was sitting with a dishevelled looking Avni. Her eyes looked pink as if she had cried earlier.

"Hey, is there a major problem?" Aakash asked without spending time with any preliminaries.

Avni looked at him. "Actually, Vivan, my son is constantly crying. It has been a few hours now. I don't know what has happened to him." She then looked away. "He is not like this normally." Aakash could see her eyes getting moist again. It was an unusual situation indeed. For a moment, the words "my son" kept revibrating in his ears, but he conveniently ignored it. It was weird for him to be drawn into something like this. This kind of emotional things never really mattered to him. But now, he didn't have much choice. It was a question of an infant. Perhaps he was not well. And as usual, his commitment to any patient was unquestioned. Moreover, he didn't like seeing Avni in such a miserable state.

"Okay, get ready, pack your bag, I will take you home." He turned, not waiting to see Avni's reaction. She quietly wiped her tears.

A beautiful summer night with cool breeze teasing the crescent moon and the twinkling stars tried to soothe her fraying nerves, but failed miserably. Traffic was minimal, and Aakash's Audi had the road all to itself. Avni sat silently. It was awkward. The man whom she preferred to avoid from day one had suddenly turned out to be her savior. Yes, her savior. After all, Vivan was her life.

"I think you are crossing the speed limit," Avni said, breaking the silence.

He gave her a sideward glance and slowed down. "I thought you would want to reach home as soon as possible," he replied in his deep voice.

"I would certainly like to. Thank you for your concern." She was pleasantly surprised at his uncharacteristic caring attitude, something she really didn't expect.

They again rode in silence for a while when Avni's phone rang again. It was Mrs Joseph. "Don't worry, I'm almost there." She could hear Mrs Joseph's sigh of relief.

"Is he any better?" She heard him asking as soon as she hung up. She could sense a speck of anxiety in his voice.

"It seems he is tired of crying now." She looked at the road ahead. "Mrs Joseph, Vivan's nanny, was saying that he wants to sleep, but can't. He gets up every now and then."

"How old is he?"

"He is going to be nine months next week."

"It might be colic pain."

They remained silent for the rest of the journey. Aakash didn't ask anything further. No uncomfortable questions about her past. She had no idea whether he knew anything about her personal life or not. He was Neha's friend. Perhaps she had told him. Or she hadn't. At this point, she didn't care. She was actually grateful for his trademark indifference tonight. *Life is much more endurable when sometimes some questions remain unasked, buried beneath the layers of silence.*

Soon they reached her house. As soon as Aakash pulled over, she jumped out.

"Be careful!" he said. He then promptly locked the car and followed her.

Mrs Joseph opened the door and led them into Vivan's room. He was half-asleep, his face was covered with dried tears, his long curly hair plastered across his face. He opened his eyes as soon as he heard them approaching. Avni instantly took him in her arms and hugged him tightly. Aakash could see tears streaming down her face.

"My baby..." Avni kissed Vivan. "You will be alright."

He inquired Mrs Joseph regarding Vivan's condition. When did the pain start? Was it constant or intermittent? What did he have for dinner?

He then turned towards Avni, who was still holding Vivan, wiping his tears and removing strands of from his face.

"Dr Avni, obviously I am not a paediatrician, but can you trust me? Can I examine the baby before making any decisions?"

"Of course! I never had any doubts about your professional acumen." She faintly smiled.

She then put Vivan down on his bed. He was not happy with a stranger touching him and started crying again, but Avni managed to pacify him. Aakash palpated his stomach. "Like I said before, it seems he has some colic pain." He looked at Mrs Joseph, "And you said the pain was intermittent? Right? Like it comes and goes?"

"Yes, exactly! He cries and is then okay and then cries again."

"Yeah, so colic pain is quite normal for infants of this age." He looked at Avni, "You should not worry. He will be okay." Then he asked, "Do you have Colimex drops at home?"

"I think I just might." She took Vivan in her arms. "Let me check, I'm hoping it hasn't expired because I think it's been sitting there for a long time."

She went to the next room and came back with a bottle of medicine. Aakash checked the expiry date and asked Avni to give Vivan five drops of it.

"Why didn't I think of this?" Avni said while giving medicine drops to Vivan. "I was getting so paranoid when Mrs Joseph was calling frantically."

"You are a mother." He looked at her, half-smiling and then looked away. "It happens; you are the worst doctor for your own child." He remembered how his own mother used to get paranoid whenever he was unwell.

Soon after, Vivan was able to sleep. It had been an exhausting day of crying, and after the relief, he experienced from the medicine, he dozed off.

"I think that we can go back to Faridabad now. Vivan seems to be okay." Her heart was beating fast as she mouthed those words. *How could she leave Vivan?* But at the same time, she did not want to come across as someone who was running away from her duties, especially in front of the person who thought her to be insincere and careless earlier.

"I think you should stay back." He looked away. "Vivan needs you. There are other people over there to take care of things. The camp can always run without you."

She was so relieved. She wanted to hug him. "Thank you so much, Dr Aakash!" she said.

"And please don't hesitate to call in case you need any help." He stepped out the door. His tone had the same quality of professionalism as when he dealt with his patients at the OPD.

He then drove away. Avni kept looking at the tail-lights of the car until they faded away from sight merging with the light of the last star in the sky as dawn descended on earth with the first few rays of the sun emerging from the horizon.

12

Time flies in happiness and in sorrow. It never stops. It never waits. It has to keep moving for the universe to reach its destiny. Avni was so busy with her residency program and raising Vivan that she never realized how quickly time went by. It was already September, bringing along a relief after the scorching summer heat and humid, rainy season. Fortunately, her parents had not only helped her in finding a lovely, three-bedroom apartment in one of the good suburbs of Delhi, but had also paid for it. It was as if the warm summer had thawed the ice between her and her parents. Although, there was still a lot to be achieved, at least there were definite signs of budding reconciliation. Although her father hadn't talked to her, he had asked for Vivan's photos when Sia had visited her recently. Her mother had given an indication that she might accompany Sia on her next trip to the city. Mrs Trivedi mostly mouthed 'Yes' and 'No' when talking on the phone, but the ice had certainly started melting. And she could feel the warmth of the forgotten adoration that her parents had for her radiating again in small ways. Sia had told her how her father got teary-eyed seeing Vivan's photo and couldn't speak for a few minutes after that. She couldn't get over how proud he looked at that moment. After listening to all this, Avni had promised Sia that she would never let them down again or would do anything to hurt their feelings. She had definitely learned from her mistake and would never repeat it.

Also, thawing were her feelings for Aakash. Not that there was any change in the way that he interacted with her for he was as professional as ever, but after the medical camp, she couldn't pretend to be so aloof. He had helped her in the mini-crisis. Because of him, her world was instantly restored. Sometimes, even a small gesture of care can create a huge difference. And that difference was also reflected in the change in her attitude towards him. At least she didn't hate him anymore. The space that was previously occupied by hate was left empty. She had no name for the feeling, though.

At the hospital, the scenario had suddenly turned chaotic as the city was under the grip of dengue fever. After the rainy season, it had almost become an annual phenomenon, but this year, it was much more aggressive. It was, once again, going to be a long night. Avni was getting ready to go to work, but was quite paranoid about Vivan. Mrs Joseph was instructed to use mosquito-repellent liberally at home. His evening strolls were curtailed for the time being as the fear of mosquito bites loomed large in her mind.

When she reached emergency, Aakash had already done the morning rounds. The team was standing at the nurse's station, discussing the cases. The people present there were precisely the same as on her first day. It was like déjà vu. She was left with an eerie feeling, a familiar sense of uncomfortable stillness. "You are late, Dr Avni!" Dr Aakash remarked as she joined the team.

"So sorry!" She looked up. He was looking the same as he had looked on her first day, unfamiliar, distant, and detached.

Nikhil was observing her. He looked at her and gestured by blinking his eyes as if to say, "Don't worry. It's all good."

The team shortly dispersed. Everyone went off to start the day that was most likely going to be eventful with dengue cases rapidly being reported from every corner of the city. Being a government hospital, nobody could be denied admission. The wards had now started to swarm with patients. Once again, a wave of strange familiarity, albeit not a pleasant one, travelled through Avni's whole body. *I am going to be extremely careful. Not taking any chances this time.*

Avni must have seen about ten patients when a woman of around her age was brought in by her husband and some family members. The patient, Nita Sharma had a history of five days of fever, headache, body ache, loss of appetite and vomiting. The temperature was not as high as it had been earlier on, but she still looked quite ill and listless. Avni advised her to get admitted. She immediately ordered a full blood count along with some other investigations. Promptly, Avni also informed Aakash that the patient's platelet count was very low. He advised that the patient needed to be moved to the ICU. He also asked Avni to personally take charge of the patient as she had already seen her and would be the most suitable to handle the case. Of course, he was there to help her whenever she needed, he told her before moving on to another patient. Avni re-examined the patient once she was moved to the ICU. Dengue Haemorrhagic Fever was the likely clinical diagnosis in her mind.

Avni called Mrs Joseph to say that she wouldn't be home for dinner. Generally, she would go back to see Vivan at dinner time, even if it was for half an hour. But tonight, it was too busy. She remained so engrossed with the patient that she forgot to eat her dinner. It was only when Aakash came for the evening rounds and asked her about it, that she remembered. She hurriedly ordered a repeat ECG which showed abnormalities. Also, an urgent echocardiogram showed dysfunction. She updated the diagnosis of Dengue Shock Syndrome (DSS) along with myocarditis and informed Aakash about it. When he came in to see the patient, he was a little surprised to see Avni in shambles. It was already past midnight, and it showed on her face, the stress of looking after a critical patient. Her hair was falling out of place, her eyes looked sunken and the color of her skin, paler than usual. He had never seen her in such disarray.

The patient remained in intractable shock, with no response to medication or intravenous hydrocortisone, and required ventilation. Despite her best efforts to stay calm, Avni could feel panic gripping her slowly. She was not able to dissociate herself from the woman's personal life, especially the fact that she had a small child. She tried to remember how they were told by Dr Kapoor at the beginning of their residency to not take any case personally.

The patient progressively deteriorated and developed Adult Respiratory Distress Syndrome (ARDS), dying shortly afterward, fifteen hours after admission. When Avni looked at the investigation results received after the patient's death, it showed positive antibodies to dengue.

Avni remembered her first day again. *The face of death never changes, it robbed someone on that day, and it would rob someone today.* But somehow she was feeling it more deeply; perhaps because she could identify with the patient more closely, being the same age as her and having a child as dependent on her mother as Vivan was. Aakash was immediately informed by the duty nurse. He promptly rushed to the ICU. As she waited for him, her eyes travelled outside the window of the ICU. Her heart sank seeing a beautiful little girl waiting for her mother. Unaware of the tragedy that had befallen her, she was playing with her father. Everything happened so quickly that it was still difficult to believe that the woman, the mother, the wife, was no more. She could feel her eyes getting moist. She knew she was not supposed to show her weakness, she had to look strong, however empty she felt on the inside.

"Avni," Aakash's deep voice broke her thoughts. She turned around to face him.

"I am sorry!" She looked at him for a moment and then looked away, "She couldn't be saved."

He could see that she was avoiding making any eye contact. Her eyes were wet.

"You should not take it personally." He touched her arm. His voice was tender, something that Avni had never heard before. "We did our best." He paused, glanced at her again. "You have been on your toes for the last eighteen hours!"

"But we still couldn't save her," Avni uttered.

"Some things are not in our hands. We are merely doctors, not god." He remembered Avni speaking the same words in the past.

"You better go and relax in the staff room." He gently touched her shoulder. "I will inform the family about her death."

Avni walked away with slow, heavy steps.

The day after, a complaint was received by the hospital from the husband of the deceased patient that due to lack of adequate care, his wife died after only a brief illness. Avni was sad, but she remained unperturbed.

"It's just natural. I guess," she said to Dr Pandey after he informed her of what had happened. "It's difficult to accept the death of someone who is so young, and that too after such a short illness."

The medical board began their inquiry regarding the case. A report was prepared and submitted promptly. When a meeting was called to discuss the incident, everything was similar to the previous time, when Mr Singh's case went in for review. The same people were seated in the meeting room.

"Dr Avni had taken exceptional care of the patients." Aakash glanced at her. "I am yet to see someone on my team who is as committed as her. Nothing more could have been done for Ms Nita Sharma. She died of DSS. Such a tragic death does affect relatives deeply, and this case is no different." He paused and then mouthed in a slow, deliberate fashion, "I suggest that Dr Avni should not take things so personally. After all, we are only doctors."

All other three looked at each other. They seemed glad that Aakash had finally understood what they already knew about Avni. The meeting was over in less than an hour.

"Thank you, Dr Aakash!" Avni said as she stood up to move towards the exit.

"You don't need to thank me, Avni." He was standing just across from her, the closest he had ever been to her. "I just stated the truth."

Their eyes met, there was no way that they could have gauged the depth of their feelings, but the infinite distance between them suddenly appeared to be finite.

It was an early morning call from Rajiv that woke up Aakash.

"Priya is coming today by the morning flight. It lands here at 10 a.m." He shouted on the phone. "And you are going to come with me to pick her up from the airport."

Aakash remembered now, in one of her calls to him, Priya had told him that she was coming home for Diwali and had also asked him to pick her up from the airport. He had forgotten it all until now.

"I forgot about it completely!"

"Out of sight is out of mind." Rajiv laughed, and then he insisted, "Priya has specifically asked for you. See man! You can't deny her request," he continued, "Get ready quickly! I am coming to pick you up soon." Rajiv hung up before Aakash had a chance to say anything.

Aakash quietly left home when Rajiv arrived, not wanting his mother to know anything about Priya's arrival. They were at the airport in forty-five minutes. Both were waiting at the arrival gate when Rajiv spotted his sister. He waved to her. Dressed casually in jeans, jacket, and boots, she looked ultra-stylish. Aakash also slowly raised his hand to signal to her. The whole time Priya was walking towards them, her eyes were on Aakash. How she had missed him. She decided that she was going to do something about it. She couldn't let this go on. Rajiv could sense how his sister's eyes were fixed on Aakash, but he chose not to say anything. He knew his friend. Aakash was always the silent kind. He would not do anything on a whim. He would take time, but once he decided on something, committed to someone, he would not turn his back on them. In his eyes, that was a good trait.

Rajiv hugged her. She hugged him back. Aakash kept looking at them without saying a word. Then she turned towards him. How much she wanted to hug him, but his arms were crossed together close to his chest.

"So, how are you?" She looked at him. "Thanks for coming!"

"Oh, don't be so formal!" He looked back, "It's my pleasure. I had to come." The irony of his words was not lost on Priya. He was asking her to not be formal, when all he was doing precisely that.

They started walking toward the parking.

"You look more like a foreigner now!" Rajiv joked.

"Oh, I am an Indian to the core." She glanced at Aakash. "And I am going to remain so." She knew about Aakash's preference for staying in India. *When you are in love, you don't care about your own feelings. You want to make the other person happy, whatever may be the cost.*

"How long are you staying?" Aakash asked her once they were inside the car. He sat next to Rajiv in the front seat. Priya sat at the back. She could see his face in the side view mirror from behind, impassive and devoid of any emotion. She wondered when she was going to see any connection between his words and his eyes. As usual, she tried to reassure herself, one day, everything would be okay, and her dreams would be a reality.

"For a month," she promptly replied.

"We are going to have a great Diwali party." Rajiv was excited.

"That's wonderful," Aakash said. "Mum will be happy that you are here for Diwali."

"You haven't told her, have you?" Priya almost shouted from behind.

Aakash smiled broadly, for the first time since she had arrived, "Of course not! Who am I to spoil the fun?"

"Yeah, I can't wait to surprise her!" She laughed. "Thanks for not spilling the beans! I will come to see her."

"You are most welcome!" Aakash said, unaware how much meaning those unintended words carried for Priya.

Rajiv slowed the car down as they approached Aakash's house.

"You sure you want to be dropped home or would you like to come with us?" Rajiv asked him.

"I'll just go home, thanks!" He looked at them. "I can't make it today, but I'll see you soon.

He got down from the car. Priya kept looking at him until he disappeared from the sight.

13

When Avni came for her usual ward rounds in the morning, she was a little surprised to find only Aakash there. Then she remembered that Nikhil, Sandeep and Sanjay were on leave. Diwali holidays were on the cards, and a lot of staff, especially the people from interstate had started going on vacation.

Both of them started the ward round. Thankfully, they were not as full. As soon as they finished seeing the last patient, Aakash spontaneously turned towards her and said, "Let's go have some coffee!" Avni looked at him. She knew that it was customary for the team to go for coffee after the rounds. She could see that he had uttered those words more as a routine rather than giving any thought to it. He looked back, sensing what Avni was thinking. "Yes, we can't let go of our routine just because others are not around." They exchanged smiles and walked towards the hospital café that was like a second home to the registrars.

Both of them walked in silence, lost in their own thoughts. It was good that the café was close to the hospital, just a two-minute walk. She was finding it a little odd, walking alone with him and felt a sense of relief when they reached there. They took a seat near the window and ordered coffee. He was the last person she would have ever thought of going out for a coffee with. She avoided his gaze and kept looking at the table when she heard him say, "Well Dr Avni, how is your residency going?"

"Pretty good, I would say!" She paused, glancing at him.

He raised his head to look at her. She was still looking down, fiddling with her earring which was shining like a celestial object under the reflection of the morning sun.

"I guess, I haven't made it easy," he said. She raised her chin and met his eyes. Now he could look clearly into her dark, deep eyes. "No, I really mean it. Especially on your first day." *Where was all this going*? Avni thought to herself. "I must apologize to you for that day."

Now she was startled. Just the other day, Neha had mentioned that he never apologized to anyone. He believed that he could do no wrong.

Avni didn't know what to say. "It's okay!" she mumbled.

"You know what Avni..." His words shocked her as it was the first time that he had addressed her without using the prefix, 'doctor'. "I am painfully pedantic when it comes to the patients, sometimes to the extent of being irrational." He heard himself saying. He was as surprised as Avni was, with himself at his own words. But he felt good. It was like an enormous weight being lifted from his chest. He had been harsh to the hapless girl. He shouldn't have blamed Avni for the death of the patient. He had seen Avni being so dedicated to the dengue patient who had died in the hospital.

"You don't need to apologize." She then looked away. "I guess it's good to be a perfectionist."

"True, but not at the cost of questioning someone's integrity." He looked at her. "I mean, blaming someone for the things that one hasn't committed." She looked back. His eyes were so bright and transparent. She couldn't find anything other than a genuine apology.

She just smiled, the same quintessential smile that had intrigued him since he saw her for the first time. It was so enigmatic; it was as if it contained a million words that were left unspoken.

"Do you like sugar with your coffee?" He asked as he handed her the sugar jar.

"Heaps of it!" She then added two spoons full of sugar to her coffee.

"You must have a strong metabolism." His eyes shone with childlike surprise. "No one could guess that you consume so much sugar by looking at you!"

It was the first time he had said anything so personal about her. It felt strange, but she didn't mind.

No one can guess so many other things about me.

His eyes met hers, his gaze lingering a little longer. "*I will not ask you anything that you don't wish to share,*" his eyes conveyed the words he couldn't. All at once, she felt relaxed; a sense of peace washing over her. Perhaps his 'I don't care attitude' was not so bad, after all.

"Have you had a chance to see the couple, the one with HIV? I sent them your way for your thesis?" His voice again had acquired the same serious tone that she had become accustomed to.

"Yes, I did. It was so shocking." She looked at him, "I can't believe that the husband had known about his HIV status for so long but never told his wife about it."

"What?" Aakash looked genuinely concerned. "And did he continue having sex with his wife?"

"Yes, he did," she said. "He suggested getting her HIV status checked only when she started having symptoms. She was quite sick for the last one month with fever, cough and diarrhea."

"What about him? Didn't he have any symptoms?"

"On the contrary, he is quite well," she said. "He is not even on antiretroviral treatment."

"I see." He looked at her and then looked away as if trying to hide from her what he was feeling inside. He was thinking about his parents and their synthetic marriage. *There is no real love in this world. Everything is just plain nonsense. That's why I don't believe in love.*

She pretended not to notice, but she wondered what was on his mind. *Why did he look so distant, so lost*? Perhaps, she just had a glimpse of only a part of him, and not a piece that was damaged, a piece that was kept carefully hidden under the garb of his arrogance.

"And the girl is so broken, not as much by the disease as by his betrayal."

"I see," he said, but Avni could tell he didn't see. He couldn't understand how it felt to be cheated, for trust once broken could never be restored. She knew how it felt. *It shakes your faith in the most brutal manner possible. It robs you of your innocence forever. It creates a permanent space for doubts that once never existed.* She knew that she would never be able to recover her old self, a person who was so trusting.

"And you know what? She is not even angry with him." Avni's eyes were glistening with unshed tears. Little did Aakash know that somewhere Avni was able to identify herself with the girl. She was not angry when she found out about Samir cheating on her; she was hurt for he was dishonest with her. She had no issues with his choices. If he had wanted to leave the marriage, she would have set him free without a word, however painful it would have been. She always believed that love couldn't be imposed upon someone.

Either it existed, or it didn't. She wouldn't have begged him for love, for him to stay in a loveless marriage. But in her world view, to be deceived was beyond any justification.

"Does that make any difference?" He felt uncomfortable looking at her. He never liked tears. His mother's predicament had ensured that. "What's important is that his wife is most likely infected with the virus." Perhaps, it was his way of diverting the discussion, to give it a medical perspective, to sound as professional as he was known for. He never believed in sentiments. It'd better be a matter of fact without getting drowned in a sea of unnecessary complexities. But deep somewhere in his heart, he couldn't get over that strange, uncomfortable feeling. He found himself empathizing with her. He had no idea what she had gone through. Neha had told him that Avni was a divorcee. He hadn't asked anything. Further, he wasn't interested. But today, perhaps for the first time in his life, he found himself concerned about someone's feelings, no matter how much he pretended otherwise.

"Yes, it doesn't make any difference." By now, she had successfully managed to absorb back those tears. "The damage has been done. Complete. Permanent." She took a deep breath. She didn't say that HIV could still be taken care of for the new drugs were doing miracles, but the damage done to her trust could never be treated. The stolen faith could never be retrieved. It had been lost forever.

He was looking at her, noticing everything about her, every curve that her mouth took, every time her eyes blinked, every word she spoke, and every breath she took. For reasons yet unknown to him, he was not able to detach himself with what she had just said. He prided himself with his 'I don't care attitude' and now, all of a sudden, it was looking so fragile. He wondered about her past. It occurred to him now that probably she was identifying with the patient's pain, the sorrow that the wife was going through.

"We can't undo what has happened to her. But let's start the treatment."

It was the first time since she had known him that she found something else in his voice, something other than the plain indifference, other than the pure professionalism. She couldn't name it yet.

After that, nothing ever remained quite the same between them.

Dr Pandey had asked Aakash and Avni to see him in his office. Avni hurriedly got ready in the morning. Vivan had now become accustomed to her routine. He was watching Scooby Doo, his favourite cartoon on the iPad. She could hear Mrs Joseph fussing over him. He didn't let anyone touch the iPad. Avni was a little worried about the amount of time he was spending on it. Her mother, who was now more amiable, had told her not to worry so much about it. Although she had still not visited Avni in Delhi, she would call on Skype almost every day. Avni knew that she wanted to see Vivan. She would call many times when Avni would be at work. She had hoped that one day her parents would forgive her. She had, in fact, kept one room reserved for them at home. She had carefully decorated the room, taking care of their needs and choice. She had also got an old framed picture of the whole family on one of the walls. Mrs Joseph was instructed to help Vivan learn how to pronounce Nana and Nani. Avni was looking forward to the day when she would finally feel redeemed when they came to visit her.

Avni was wearing a beautiful turquoise blue saree, coordinated with a turtle neck jumper of the same colour. Her hair was tied up with a few strands loosely hanging from the sides. She checked the time in the car radio as she started the engine. She was ten minutes behind schedule. Avni wondered what the meeting was about. *Perhaps, it's about my thesis work. It's been a long time since he's talked to me about it.* She parked the car and then hurriedly walked towards the medicine department, heading straight to Dr Pandey's room.

Avni reached his office and slowly opened the door to step inside. She was closing the door behind her when she saw Aakash. He was sitting there, engrossed in looking at his phone. He looked up and smiled. She smiled back. Perhaps for the first time since she had joined the hospital, there was an implicit spontaneity between them.

"What a pleasant surprise." He couldn't stop himself from silently admiring her beauty. She looked much better when not so stressed, he thought.

"Hi! You're here to see Dr Pandey too?" She pulled out a chair for herself. "I'm guessing he wants to discuss my thesis."

"I think so." He kept his phone in the jacket's pocket.

"I hope he hasn't found too many problems with my work."

Aakash smiled. "You are doing good work. You should not worry."

"Thanks, Dr Aakash." She remembered the days when he would find fault in whatever she did. *At least I can work peacefully now.*

Her eyes then travelled to the door that had just opened when she saw Dr Pandey walking in.

"Good morning!" He glanced at both of them. "Hope you haven't been waiting too long."

"Good morning!" Both of them greeted back.

He took his seat. He signed a few papers that his secretary had brought in and then looked up.

"So, the reason I called both of you today is this..." His eyes moved from Aakash to Avni and then back. "There is an AIDS charity program organized by SMILE this Saturday night, the charity that works for children whose parents have died of AIDS."

Avni nodded her head. She knew these kids very well as they came in for regular check-ups and Avni had become quite close to some of them.

He continued, "I am going to Mumbai for a meeting. I am wondering if you two could attend it." He glanced at Avni, "I don't want to disappoint them."

"That would be great! I would certainly like to go." Aakash's prompt reply took Dr Pandey by surprise. There was no denying that his words matched his demeanor. For the first time, Dr Pandey noticed that instead of the usual plain indifference to anything even slightly outside his professional domain, his eyes shone with genuine interest.

Avni was still silent, looking down at the table and fiddling with her pen. Both of them were looking at her with curiosity. After a pause, Dr Pandey asked, "Is it possible for you to go, Dr Avni?"

She could feel Aakash's eyes on her. She uttered with a little hesitation, "If you want it, I will certainly go."

"You know Dr Avni," Dr Pandey said, "Mrs Malhotra, the chairman of SMILE has specifically asked for you. She has told me how close you have become to these children."

"Thanks, sir!" She said. "I would be nice to see them perform."

Aakash was observing her, waiting anxiously for her to agree. He sighed with relief.

"That's wonderful!" Dr Pandey said, "I will inform them that you two will be representing me."

"You should go with Aakash," Neha told Avni when they met at the cafeteria during lunch. "You are not well versed with the geography of the city. This place, the theatre where the program is supposed to be held, is a little difficult to find."

"I should be alright," Avni said in a hesitant tone. She didn't want to go with Aakash. Although he had been quite nice when Dr Pandey had proposed the plan in the morning, she still felt uneasy. It was okay when he drove her from the medical camp the other night when Vivan was not well. It was more of an emergency situation then. Now she didn't feel the need. But before Neha could have said anything, she saw Aakash walking towards them.

"Hi, Aakash!" Neha waved to him, "So good to see you! It has been ages."

He waved back. There was a smile on his face. He approached the table where they were sitting and glanced at Avni.

"Can I join you guys?"

"Of course! Funny, we were just talking about you." Neha offered him the chair next to her. Avni looked at him as he sat down. He looked so handsome, she thought.

For a reason yet unknown to him, he found it so elating that he was a topic of their conversation that Avni was also part of.

"I hope it wasn't anything bad." He glanced at Avni, "I doubt she has any good things to say about me."

Avni instantly found herself blushing. He was watching her. She shook her head, "Of course not! There isn't anything bad to say about you."

"I have been too harsh with her." Aakash smiled at Avni.

"I would take it as serious mentoring." Neha laughed. "It's alright, it all worked out at the end. Now you have a better understanding of each other's work."

Aakash wasn't sure if he would ever understand her correctly, but nodded his head and smiled.

"Anyway, I was telling Avni that she should go with you to the charity function." Neha looked at Aakash, "Is that okay with you?"

"It would be my pleasure."

Not knowing exactly 'why' but Avni changed her mind. "Thank you, I'd really appreciate it," she said. "I hate driving at night, and my knowledge of the city is limited."

"And GPS doesn't always help!" Neha added with a laugh.

"No worries at all. I'll pick you up."

The next day, Aakash was at Avni's house at seven in the evening. Mrs Joseph answered the doorbell with Vivan tailing her. Aakash kneeled down to greet the little boy. Vivan tried to hide behind Mrs Joseph. "He is a little shy, especially if he is meeting someone for the first time," she said.

"But it's not my first time." Aakash smiled. "I have met him before. Remember when he had an upset tummy?"

"Oh, yes! Then he should be able to recognize you. He has a sharp memory."

Both of them then turned to look at Vivan. She was right. Vivan was smiling at Aakash. His beautiful angelic face was a replica of Avni's. His curly golden brown hair was carelessly scattered all over his forehead. The bright, transparent eyes had so much innocence in them. Aakash extended his hand, "Hello, young man!"

Vivan promptly extended his little hand. Aakash shook hands with him and gently patted his back. Vivan's radiant smile instantly melted his heart. He smiled and lifted him in his arms. Mrs Joseph was eyeing them secretly and loved the bonding between them, but she maintained a straight face. "I'll let Avni know you're here."

Aakash was playing with Vivan when Avni appeared. Momentarily, she paused and kept looking at them. Vivan was always a playful child, but the way he was enjoying himself with Aakash was surprising. And what was even more surprising was seeing Aakash in such a lively mood.

"Hi Dr Aakash!" she said making him turn to look at her. "It looks like Vivan has made a new friend." She smiled.

"Definitely!" Aakash said as he handed Vivan to Mrs Joseph. "He is a lot of fun. If not for the program, I would have loved to spend some more time with him."

"You are welcome anytime." Avni heard herself saying before she could realize. After ages, she was as spontaneous as she used to be in her early days. How could she be so careless? She didn't share that kind of friendship with him.

"Yes, I must see him again," he said, thankfully not noticing her uneasiness.

Both of them waved goodbye to Vivan and Mrs Joseph. To Avni's relief, Vivan didn't throw any tantrums. He seemed to be slowly adjusting to her schedule.

They got in the car. Avni looked beautiful in a cherry red silk saree. Aakash could smell the floral scent of her perfume which was subtly intoxicating. He thought of complimenting her but then changed his mind. He had praised women before, but somehow it felt like it was the first time he was interacting with a woman at such a personal level. He felt utterly clueless as to what to say.

They kept driving in silence for some time when he mustered some courage, "Tell me about yourself. Like, about your life before coming here."

Avni thought about her carefree days as a graduate and then how all of a sudden, everything that mattered to her was so brutally crushed in just a matter of a year.

She glanced at him. "I was doing MBBS." *I was someone else.*

He smiled, "Of course, I know that!" He gave her a sideward glance without taking his eyes off the road, "That's why you are here, to do post-graduation now. Right?"

Avni felt a sense of relief that he didn't notice what she was thinking.

"Yes, I mean, doing MBBS was the main thing. Rest was all ordinary, nothing extraordinary to mention." She was lying. It was all so extraordinary. She chose to ruin her beautiful, comfortable life that had everything one could ask for, by marrying Samir on an impulse. And from there, everything was downhill until Vivan was born and then her relocation to Delhi, a place that was helping her in blurring the painful memories of those dark days.

"Isn't the ordinariness of life all that we want? Isn't that where happiness lies?" he asked.

"I guess so." She had no idea why he was saying all this. *Was it his own experience? But that was impossible with the kind of extraordinary life he had led with the best of everything in the world at his disposal.*

After that, both remained silent for the rest of the journey. Avni was happy that Aakash didn't ask anything further that could make her uncomfortable. She started to remember the days that had turned her life upside when suddenly her ordinary life had turned extraordinary. Vivan was just a month old. Samir was home after a week-long business trip. Avni decided to confront him. She knew he had been cheating on her. But just to give him the benefit of the doubt, or perhaps pitting the last ray of hope against her conviction, she asked: "Is it true?"

She waited for an answer with bated breath, to hear that it was not right, that she was so wrong. She had misunderstood him and there was no space for mistrust in their marriage.

"Yes, it is," he said gingerly. She listened to the words she was hoping to be false. But then, it registered, slowly, painfully that her conviction had finally won against her hope.

After what seemed like an eternity, she spoke.

"You could have told me that you didn't love me. You can't be held in prison against your own wish and that you think you deserved someone better."

He had expected anything from her but this. Her tone was flat. There was no emotion, no sign of accusation, anger, denial or pain. She seemed very calm. It was as if they were making holiday plans and having their usual differences.

"I didn't want to hurt you."

She had desperately tried to find meaning in those empty and hollow words which were dissolving even before they had reached her, for she wanted to believe in them. For her sake. For his sake. For the sake of love, she believed they once shared. But she couldn't. The irony of those words was not lost on her. And then, in the middle of the night, she had picked up Vivan from his crib and walked off to an unknown future, a future that was little less ordinary, full of uncertainties and darkness.

"We are here." Aakash's voice suddenly broke her thought process. He bought her back to the present when he parked the car and turned to look at her, "Are you alright? You seem to be lost."

"I'm alright, thanks!" He then got out of his seat and came around to open the door for her.

They walked towards the auditorium together where they were welcomed by the chairman, Mrs Malhotra and then ushered to sit in the front row. Avni knew a lot of children who were participating. She was in regular touch with them and knew most of them by name. In fact, whenever she would feel low, she would take inspiration from these children. They were not only orphaned but were also infected with HIV, and yet were still so cheerful and optimistic in life.

Avni was enthralled by the spectacle in front of her and Aakash had turned to look at her, enchanted by her enchantment. He was getting hopelessly and helplessly attracted to her. The program finished at around 10 p.m. Avni was overwhelmed when she heard her name being called out for the prize distribution. His eyes followed her as she walked on to the stage. He smiled when Avni shyly presented the award. *I have yet to meet such a down to earth girl. She looked all the more pretty as she blushed.* He clapped loudly. He had attended so many cultural evenings, he thought, but for the first time, he felt so joyful.

On the way back to the parking lot, he noticed her shivering in the cold Delhi night. She didn't have anything warm on her, "Are you cold?"

"Yeah, silly me, not wanting to wear a jacket because it didn't match my saree." She smiled. "But it's okay, we'll be inside the car soon."

But before they could have walked any further, Aakash took off his jacket and offered it to her. She was surprised, but she didn't protest as he placed his jacket over her shoulders. She suddenly felt warm and secure.

On the way back, they talked about the children, their life, struggles and their hopes against despair. Avni had never seen him so lively. After ages, Aakash felt like he was part of something meaningful, he felt really content. It was like he had found the core of his existence that was at peace with itself. All the hankering, all the restlessness, the entire burden of the façade that he was carrying around seemed to disappear. He had no idea if it was because of Avni or the program that he attended, but it didn't matter, he was happy.

They reached Avni's house. He parked the car outside the gate when unexpectedly she heard him asking, "Hope you don't mind, but can I ask you something?"

"Sure," she said hesitatingly, having no idea what he was going to say.

"Are you a divorcee?" He had heard it from Neha, but he wanted to ask her himself.

She looked at him. His expression was as professional as it used to be in the hospital, completely detached. It was like he was asking a patient about her marital history.

"Yes, I am." Her answer was equally professional. No change in the tone of her voice. He looked at her and said, "It takes a lot of courage to walk out of a bad marriage." He paused. "Not everyone can show such courage. I admire you."

His words sounded so sincere. Avni wondered how someone who was not even in that situation could understand her so well. She had yet to learn a lot about him, about his mother and the pain that she had endured.

"It's not easy, but I am trying to learn to live on my own." She found herself sharing her feelings.

"I understand."

"Anyway, thanks for giving me a lift."

"Anytime!" He waved her goodbye. She waved back.

He waited for her to enter the house and kept looking at her as she disappeared behind the door before driving off.

Aakash was having breakfast in the morning before going to the hospital when his mother also joined him. His mother, Dr Puja, was in her late fifties but no one could guess her age by simply looking at her. Her elegance had successfully managed to conceal the painful realities of her life that she had endured almost all her married life. How many times had she wanted to get out of the difficult marriage, but somehow couldn't gather enough courage to do so? And every time she didn't leave a husband who would beat her mercilessly in a fit of rage, she gave him tactical permission to do it again. It was absurd that she had been living like this for the last twenty-five years. After every episode of the beating, he would turn into the best husband in the world. He asked for her forgiveness, and she felt a strange sense of righteousness in being a wronged woman. She would let it go, and the vicious cycle would continue.

The couple had successfully kept it hidden from Aakash for quite long, but he started seeing their complicated relationship as soon as he entered his teenage years. Initially, it was quite puzzling for him, seeing those blue-black areas on her mother's arms, but gradually he started understanding. He wondered if it was because of him that she stayed with his difficult father. She could have left him easily otherwise. She was a financially independent woman, a well-known doctor who could have had an army of lawyers to represent her case. Perhaps, people become conditioned to bad things in life, he would think to himself. He had persistently avoided talking about this with his mother. And there was no question of talking to his father, a strict father who had always managed to drive him away.

However, by not expressing all of his anger and frustration didn't mean that he wasn't affected by all this. Talking about it would have eased his pain, diluted his trauma, vented out his anger. But, instead, he had gradually drawn into a shell that gave him immunity from the world. His mother remembered how her soft-spoken, mild-natured teenage son had steadily turned into an arrogant adult. His arrogance was a way of dealing with his pain. He didn't want to be close to anyone. All his close friends except for Rajiv gradually disappeared from his life. What remained was a crowd of superficial people around him. The so-called "friends" who just wanted to have a good time. He would party till late on most weekends, perhaps just to forget himself. His mother had observed with pain how her son had started drinking so much. She tried to talk him out of it, trying to pretend that everything was alright in her marriage, that they were very blessed, that they were one of the best families, but it didn't work. The truth could not be resurrected on a foundation of lies. Mrs Mehta's only other hope was Priya, she believed Priya was the only girl who could really understand Aakash and would make him happy if they got married.

"Good morning!" Mrs Mehta beamingly greeted her son.

"Good morning Mum!" He looked at her.

"Priya called yesterday." She glanced at him half expecting him to be curious. He wasn't. He kept eating from the bowl of cereal, looking down. "You must be aware of the Diwali party at Rajiv's house."

"Yes. Rajiv told me about it." He sounded disinterested, but perhaps for the sake of his mother, kept talking about it.

"I hope you are going. Priya specifically asked me to remind you."

"I guess…I have to check the hospital roster." He was tentative. "Well, anyway, I am sure you and Dad will be going."

"Yes, we are. But you should also come." His mother was persistent.

"Of course! I will certainly try." He tried to infuse some conviction in his voice. He hated disappointing his mother. He would invariably try to make her happy. He used to enjoy the annual Diwali celebration, but gradually over the years, he had started realizing the futility of it all. The loud music and food were all there to please the senses, but it couldn't give him any lasting joy or contentment. In fact, after meeting Avni, that feeling was getting stronger. He admired her simple life that she was trying to carve out for herself after her tumultuous marriage. It was not easy to be a divorcee in this country, but she was strong enough to live her life amidst the storm. He felt so peaceful when he was with her. It was as if he had found his much-desired serenity. Her sublime presence would make him forget his loneliness that had become his constant companion. Avni didn't speak much, but he didn't need to hear her to feel happy or at ease. Her silence was equally enchanting.

They finished eating their breakfast in silence after that, both avoiding speaking about the obvious, Priya.

14

Aakash had just finished his OPD when he spotted Avni at the staff coffee room. Although he didn't want to look at her, he couldn't help himself. Her ethereal beauty was so captivating. Whatever little he had learned about her from Neha, he admired the way she had been managing her life.

"How are you?" he asked her.

"I am good." She smiled. "Not many patients in the ward."

"Yeah, it's good. What are your plans for Diwali?"

"Nothing much…Vivan. Mrs Joseph and I will probably have our own little celebration." As an afterthought, Avni added, "My younger sister Sia was supposed to join us. But she had to go overseas to attend a business meeting."

"I see." He glanced at her face, trying to see if she looked okay. He had no idea why he wanted to see her happy, make sure that she was not feeling alone and was well over her past, whatever it was.

"I wish she could have been here. It's our second Diwali with Vivan. He is now a little grown up to understand the celebrations; he was very small when it was his first Diwali." For the first time, she expressed her feelings in front of him. And for the first time, he saw a tinge of sadness on her face. He wanted to ask her about her parents, but resisted. Over the years, perhaps because of the complicated situation at his own home, he had learned not to interfere or ask too much about other people's lives.

"Anyway, do you want some coffee?" she asked.

"Yes please, thanks!"

Avni handed him the mug. They talked about a few patients and then it was time to leave.

"Happy Diwali Avni," he said. "Hope you have a good time."

"Thanks and same to you as well, Dr Aakash! I am sure you are going to have a blast."

As they went their separate ways, Aakash thought about not seeing her for almost a week. And suddenly, just like that, it hit him then how Avni had slowly occupied such a large part of his life.

The next evening was one of the biggest celebrations at Rajiv's home. Diwali was always celebrated with much zest and fervor at the Kapoor residence, but this year, it carried more significance as Priya was back from London during her study break. Being well aware of the fact that his sister liked Aakash, Rajiv wanted to make this a memorable event for her. He knew that Aakash's parents were very fond of Priya. He was also sure that Aakash liked his sister, but was unable to express his feelings for her.

Rajiv was all set to give his sister one of the best presents she could ask for this Diwali. He was going to tell Aakash to marry his sister. Both the set of parents were equally excited at this idea, for they felt it was the right time and occasion for it. Added to the fact, Mrs Mehta had indicated to Priya only a few days back that off late, Aakash hadn't shown any apparent resistance to the idea of getting married. This just added onto Rajiv's desire to finally push Aakash to take the plunge.

The house was traditionally lit up with a lot of attention to detail. It seemed as if stars had descended from the sky with twinkling fairy lights all around. Dressed to kill, Priya looked beautiful in a pink lehenga. She stared at her reflection in the mirror a little longer than usual and was pleased with herself, all the while wondering what Aakash would think, the one man she had dressed so carefully for

Mr and Mrs Kapoor were welcoming guests. When Mr and Mrs Mehta arrived, they were overjoyed to see them. These days they hadn't been attending too many social events and to have them come over was a pleasant surprise. Priya eyed them from a distance. She figured Aakash would be on his way too.

Drinks had started with an ample supply of delicious entrées served by waiters moving amongst the thick lawns. A dance event was also scheduled for the evening. Priya was going to participate. In fact, she was the star attraction. She had painstakingly learned the dance steps, some of which were almost unmanageable for her. But she didn't mind. There was still no sign of Aakash. Priya's eyes had not left the entrance door even for a second. She would greet every guest, her smile getting fainter with every passing minute, her eyes scanning every person as they came in.

"It's not unusual with him," Rajiv said to her when he noticed her getting restless. "He is known for his idiosyncrasies."

Priya smiled weakly, "I guess!" She paused for a moment. "He might be busy with his patients."

"Should I call him?" Rajiv asked.

"We should wait." She looked at her brother, "He might not like it."

Why does she care so much about his feelings when he didn't even bother to show up on time? Rajiv was getting increasingly frustrated but didn't say anything to his sister.

It was now time for the dance performance. And still, Aakash was nowhere in sight. Very reluctantly, Priya went ahead to perform, hoping against hope that he would turn up soon. Her parents could sense how distracted she looked. Mrs Mehta could see her anxiety too. She had tried to call Aakash on his mobile phone a few times, but there was no response.

The dance was about to finish when Rajiv's phone rang. He was relieved to see Aakash's name flash on the screen. He promptly picked up the phone. *He must have been stuck with some patient, an emergency perhaps.*

"Sorry, Rajiv." Aakash's deep voice echoed from the other side.

"Where are you?" Rajiv almost barked, "We all are waiting for you. Priya is getting impatient."

After a pause, he said, "I won't be able to make it. Something has come up." That was it. Rajiv knew from the way he said it, that he didn't want any further questions. He didn't tell him that at this very moment, he was at Avni's house, that he was on his way to the party but then decided to turn his car around and drive in the opposite direction. He thought of Avni and Vivan being alone today, on Diwali. He didn't feel like partying it up when Avni was feeling sad because her sister couldn't join her for the night.

Avni was playing with Vivan in her bedroom when she heard a knock at the door. She asked Mrs Joseph to check. It must be one of those people who come looking for Diwali charity. She was feeling very lonely. Sia's last minute change had made things worse. Routine life was okay, but on occasions like Diwali, when everyone was celebrating, when even the air was loaded with a festive odour, it was almost impossible not to miss family. She rued what 'family' meant for her. She was a divorcee, a single woman with a child. No husband or in-laws. Her parents were slowly adjusting to the new reality. And the only person close to her, her sister, was far off attending a meeting in San Francisco.

"It's Dr Aakash," Mrs Joseph informed her after she opened the door. Generally Mrs Joseph didn't open the door for anyone unknown as she followed a strict security protocol put in place by Avni, but she knew Aakash very well now. As soon as Avni heard his name, she was startled. *Why is he here and that too today, a holiday? Could it be an emergency? But he could have just called me.*

She had no make-up on, her hair was a mess, and she was still in her track pants. For a moment she thought about changing, but then decided otherwise. She took Vivan in her arms and walked towards the lounge. Vivan was excited, he loved having visitors. And there he was, standing with his back towards Avni, busy looking at the framed photograph of her and Vivan. Sia had beautifully captured a candid moment with Avni tenderly looking at Vivan sleeping. It was one of Avni's most treasured possessions. Sometimes, she would sit by herself and keep looking at it for a long time. Every time Avni looked at the photograph, she would attest to the fact that she had been so fortunate to have given birth to Vivan.

On hearing footsteps, he turned. Avni's heart skipped a beat. *He's so incredibly handsome.* He looked at her. Her simple, girl-next-door appearance instantly put him at ease. He felt strangely comfortable, unlike how he would have felt around the high society girls at the Diwali party. Her eyes had questions, and he had no answers to those questions. He had no idea why he was here instead of going to Rajiv's party. Why he couldn't bear to have Avni feel lonely tonight.

"Dr Aakash!" Avni's surprise was evident in her tone. "All well? Is there an emergency at the hospital?"

"All well Avni!" He tried his best to hide his dilemma of being there, uninvited. "Just thought of greeting you on Diwali."

"Thank you!" Avni was still perplexed, but she succeeded in pretending otherwise. "Thanks for visiting us."

She offered him a seat on the sofa. Vivan, in the meantime, had managed to get out of her grasp and crawled to Aakash's side, trying to stand with his support.

"I remember you telling me that your sister was supposed to be here for Diwali, but couldn't make it. So I thought I could give you guys some company," he said in his effort to diffuse the awkwardness.

"Oh, that's really sweet of you!" She heard herself replying. He had thought of her being alone with Vivan on the night of a festival. In spite of her not wanting to, she thought of Samir abandoning her on the night of Vivan's birth.

"So how are you all celebrating?" He looked at Vivan, who was now sitting next to him on the sofa. She knew how much it would have taken him to visit them. He wouldn't have done it if he could have helped it. And for that, she couldn't help but appreciate his gesture.

"Nothing much!" She tried to avoid looking at him. "Some candles and a few crackers." Then, as if remembering something, she called out to Mrs Joseph and asked her to get some sweets for Aakash.

"Nice. Why don't we decorate the house too? It seems you haven't really started yet." He then looked at her expectantly, waiting for her to accept his offer.

She smiled back. "I haven't even changed my clothes, still in pajamas."

"Okay. Go and change. Hurry up!" His authority resembled the way he ordered things to get done at the hospital. But she didn't mind. In fact, she felt a strange sense of belonging.

As he waited for Avni, he sat down with Vivan, who wanted Aakash to play with his Lego blocks. Mrs Joseph stood in the corner watching them. Vivan was laughing, handing over the blocks to Aakash one by one and he slowly joined them to make a structure out of them. Both of them were so engrossed in no time that no one noticed Avni re-appearing. She called out to let them know. "Okay, I am ready!" She said. "Let's start doing up this place!"

Aakash raised his head from the blocks to look at her. She looked gorgeous. The color of her orange sari reminded him of the rising sun that he would have a glimpse of from his bedroom window when sometimes he would wake up a little too early in the morning. He could not take his eyes off of her. Vivan was tugging at his leg. "He wants your complete attention," Mrs Joseph said smilingly. "These days he is becoming quite demanding."

Avni picked Vivan up. "Okay baby! We will play later." She kissed him.

All three of them, Aakash, Avni and Mrs Joseph started decorating the house with candles. Aakash painstakingly hanged a couple of decorative light strings outside. Vivan clapped his little hands together, happy at this flurry of exciting activities. He was so delighted that for a moment Avni couldn't stop herself from feeling guilty of depriving him of his father. But then the thought of Samir touched her raw, unhealed pain of being wronged.

With much effort, she tried to escape those memories from her mind. Her eyes caught Aakash stealing a glance at her. It was the first time since she had met him that she noticed a sense of ardency in his eyes. She could feel her cheeks getting red. In spite of knowing that this was not her path, that she was not destined for it, she felt a strange sense of pull. Instantly, she brushed aside the feeling, wondering if she was wrong in letting go of her mask of aloofness that she had been able to wear for so long. Her reverie broke when she heard Aakash, "Decorations done!"

"Thank you!" Avni said, "If you like, you can join us for the puja."

Aakash instantly agreed. Mrs Joseph looked at them surreally as he joined Avni and Vivan for the puja. How beautiful all three of them looked together, she thought.

After the puja, Avni asked him if he would like to stay for the dinner, but he said that he had to attend a friend's party. To her surprise, she didn't want him to go yet. At least, because of him, Vivan could see what a Diwali celebration looked like. Because of him, she wouldn't go to bed crying, cursing her past and regretting about her choices in life. But she didn't say anything. She said, "Thanks Dr Aakash, you have made our day!" She looked at Vivan, "Look, how happy he is!"

"My pleasure!" He smiled, "One favor though, can you please not call me Dr Aakash? How about just Aakash?"

She smiled. "I will try!"

Then he gently kissed Vivan on his forehead and left after waving her goodbye.

As he started the engine, suddenly he didn't feel like going to Rajeev's party. Instead, he decided to go home. After a long time, he felt so content. He didn't want to spoil the sublimity of it all by going to the noisy party, a place where Priya was perhaps still waiting for him. As he drove, he saw the city decorated like a new bride, glittering with lights on a no moon night.

❖

It was a week after Diwali. It was the first time in his whole life that Mrs Mehta had maintained a grudging distance from her son. She was upset with him for not coming to the party, and it bothered her more that he let Priya down, her prospective daughter-in-law. Even his father was not speaking with him. This didn't matter to Aakash, as they hardly talked anyway. But to have this coldness with his mother was getting a little unbearable. He loved her and was overpowered with guilt. It was the first time in his life that he had not listened to his mother. He doubted if this would be the last.

He noticed that she was not very comfortable with things being this way and was looking to end the discord albeit expecting Aakash to apologize to her. Aakash had no problems seeking forgiveness from her. After all, she was all he had. But what bothered him was something else. What if his mother asked him to apologize to Priya? She liked her too much, and Aakash was afraid that she would be unreasonable with him because of Priya.

The next morning, at the breakfast table, Aakash finally tried to end the impasse.

"Mum, can you drop me at the hospital today?" He looked at his mother, "My car is going for servicing."

Mrs Mehta looked back, her eyes full of love but a little disappointment too. "Okay! I can take you. How are you going to come back then? Do you want to be picked up too?"

Aakash let out a sigh of relief. At least she was talking politely to him. Sigh! mother's love. They just can't hold anything against you for too long.

"That would be a bonus!" He said smilingly. "Thanks, Mum!" For a moment, he thought of apologizing about that night, but then decided not to. It was perhaps better to let the contentious issue sleep. Priya was her soft spot. His mother would give him a long lecture about how Priya was hurt, that he shouldn't have disappointed her. Sometimes an unresolved truce is better than a resolved one, for efforts in resolving cause more conflict, he thought.

The hospital was crazy busy that day. With winter setting in, the number of patients arriving at the outpatient clinic was phenomenally high. Aakash hardly had time for lunch, having to attend to an emergency patient who was admitted with acute myocardial infarction. When he finally got free in the evening, he checked his phone. There were three missed calls from his mother. Suddenly he remembered that he didn't have his car today and she was supposed to pick him up. He then checked his voice messages. His mum had left a message that she was busy with an obstetric case at her private nursing home and may need to perform a cesarean section. And that she had asked Priya to pick him up. He listened to the message again. Yes, she had said Priya. The evening of the Diwali party came flashing back to his mind. Before he could think of what to do, he found her standing at the door of his cubicle. It seemed as though she had been waiting there forever, waiting for him to notice her and to know what she felt for him.

"Oh! Priya!" He tried to avoid her gaze, "Sorry, just checked these messages from mum. Hope you haven't been waiting for long."

Yes, I have been waiting for you as long as I can remember.

"No, it's okay!" She cleared her throat, "Just came ten minutes ago. I couldn't find you, though."

"Actually I was in the emergency department." He glanced at her. She looked pretty in a pink sari. Her hair was pulled back in a neat ponytail. But something was amiss from her face. He couldn't guess what it was. "It was quite a hectic day. Thank you for coming to pick me up!"

"You are always welcome!" What he couldn't guess from her face, he guessed from her voice. There was a hint of disappointment, a little sadness in her voice. And he knew the reason. He decided to apologize to her on the way home. Perhaps they could stop at a restaurant for a cup of coffee and have a little chit-chat. She might feel better once she got it out of her system. Things hurt for long if they don't get an outlet. Priya was a sweet girl. He didn't want to see her in a bad mood. He knew she was pretending that everything was okay, but on the inside, she was sad. He had not given her that kind of power over him that she could be angry. Otherwise, she would have indeed lost it at him.

"Let's go!" He gestured as he collected his jacket. "I am excited to get a ride in your posh Porsche," he said in his effort to divert her attention.

"Anytime!" She smiled for the first time.

Aakash got in the passenger seat. She pressed the ignition button and turned to look at him, "Home?"

"Would you like to have some coffee? There is this new place on the way back, Brunetti."

"Sure!" Suddenly she sounded lively. "Thanks!"

For a moment, she forgot all about her sadness. She couldn't have asked for more. He is so nice. *He couldn't have missed the party without reason. Something pressing must have come up. There's no point discussing the past. He is making it up to me. And that's more than enough.*

They reached the coffee shop within a few minutes. Priya chose a beautiful little corner to sit and ordered coffee for them. Aakash was happy that she was back to her natural self by being chatty, vibrant and was smiling.

"Sorry about that night!" He looked at her. "I couldn't make it to the party!" Priya looked at him. His clear transparent eyes seemed so genuine.

She thought about how she felt on that day, how she had cried alone in the bathroom. It was like someone had scooped her heart out and left her to die. She loved him so much that it was impossible to not feel what she was feeling. But she tenderly looked at him and said, "It's okay, I understand."

Aakash felt so relieved. "I am going to make up for it. I'll organize a family get-together for both of our families, maybe a picnic. What say?"

Her heart was filled with warmth. She could've hugged him.

"You know what would be the best way to make it up to me?" she said steadily.

"Oh, tell me!" He said enthusiastically, "Ready to do anything to compensate."

"Then propose to me Aakash," Her breath was uneven. "I have been waiting for you for so long," she said looking into his eyes.

"What?" Aakash blurted out, his ears were burning. "Are you serious?"

She just nodded her head with her eyes fixed on him. He looked shocked, but it didn't matter. Priya didn't mind. She couldn't keep waiting.

He kept looking at her and then slowly and deliberately said, "You know Priya, you are a lovely girl. I am fortunate to have you in my life. Mum is so fond of you." He paused. "But Priya, I don't love you." He knew how difficult it was for him to utter those words, but he didn't have a choice. He had to be honest.

Priya looked at him with bloodshot eyes. The pain was too evident on her face. "So, I am a very nice person. Your mum also likes me. But I am not good enough for you?"

He was looking down at the table. *He had hurt her feelings, but what could he have done. He couldn't lie or bluff anymore.*

"Anyway, remember this." She was now hysterical, "I can't stop loving you. You are the only one I have ever loved in my life." And then she rose and left the shop in a hurry. He sat there for a while, trying to think if he could have handled it otherwise. But he couldn't find any alternate options. This was the only way.

He called for a taxi and left to go home. He thought about Avni. He was now convinced he loved her, and for that one person, he was rejecting the world, not knowing if she had any feelings for him, if she could trust anyone ever again after what she had been through. But whatever it was, he was willing to wait for her, for her love.

15

"Listen! You are going." Sia was on the phone talking to Avni. "I will come over to stay with Vivan. It's just a matter of three days."

"The thing is...." Avni was cut off by her sister.

"The thing is, now Vivan is old enough. You just can't let go of such opportunities. It's important for your career."

There was silence at the other end. After not hearing anything for a bit, Sia almost shouted, "Are you listening?"

"Yes," Avni replied in an anxious voice, "but I get worried about Vivan."

"Don't you trust me? It's not Mrs Joseph. I'll be there to look after him. I am applying for leave at work.

"Okay, as you say." Avni had now surrendered to her sister. Her HIV related dissertation work had been selected for the Best Paper award at a prestigious conference to be held at Goa. She wondered if it was her father who had asked Sia to be so insistent. He always wanted her to excel in her field, to see her at the top and he believed that she could do wonders. Lately, although they still weren't talking, he had started taking a keen interest in her career, through Sia.

Sia promptly arrived on time to infuse some enthusiasm in Avni. It had been very long since she had travelled. The last time was with Samir. They had gone to Switzerland for their honeymoon. She thought about how he could afford that kind of lavish holiday but sadly couldn't afford to have a faithful relationship. She wondered if she saw streaks of his traits during the honeymoon itself. He hardly looked like he was newly married, like he was in love. He was so distracted all the time. It seemed as if the challenge was over for him, that he had acquired what he wanted and was now looking for something new. She had noticed him eyeing other girls, but she brushed aside these thoughts. She wondered how life would have been if she hadn't met him.

"Have you packed your bag?" Sia asked. "Don't just pack formal business clothes. Take something casual too."

Avni smiled at her little sister. *How their roles had reversed over the years.*

"And don't worry about Vivan at all," Sia said as she sipped her tea. "He won't even miss you with me around."

"That I am sure of!" Avni said as she rose to kiss her sister on her forehead. "You are my rock, after all."

"So how many of you are going?" Sia asked.

"Actually a lot of us, it's the same hospital team," she said without elaborating. Neha, Aakash, Nilesh, Shiv and Ankit were coming along. Lately, she was trying not to mention anything about Aakash in front of Sia. She had sensed a gradual change in his attitude and liked it. She had no idea what changed him and whatever it was, she wanted to avoid discussing anything about it with Sia. *She would be quick to judge, to interpret his intentions, his behaviour. Her one mistake had put her at the receiving end of advices and life lessons.* She loved Sia, but she wasn't ready as of yet for all that. She was happy to maintain a friendly relationship with Aakash but without any complications.

It was five in the evening when Avni left for the airport after checking every little detail about Vivan. Sia joked at her paranoia, to which she replied that she needed to be a mother to understand her feelings. Sia smiled and hugged her, reassuring that although she hadn't experienced motherhood, Vivan was like her own son.

Avni met up with the rest of the team at the airport. Neha looked genuinely happy to see her, "Thank god, you made it!"

Shiv Mathur congratulated her for the award. "I am so impressed with you!"

Nilesh joked, "Beauty with brains!"

Everyone had something to say about the trip, except Aakash. He was sitting silently, busy with his phone. Every now and then, he would look in their direction, specifically stealing glances at Avni. He wouldn't have attended the conference, if not for Avni. He never liked such gatherings; he found them to be a senseless waste of resources that could have been used for providing much-needed support to poor patients living with HIV/AIDS. But when he found out that Avni was going, he instantly agreed to join them, much to Neha's surprise.

The first day went off very well. Avni got her award, and everyone congratulated her. But it was Aakash's words that made her feel really good, "It's so good to see your transformation from an unsure, hesitant registrar to such a promising young doctor."

"Thanks, Aakash! I am so happy."

He smiled and kept looking at her without saying anything. The glint in her eyes was in sync with what she had just said. He reflected on how much she had changed since she had joined the hospital.

She smiled back. She wondered if this was what she had wanted all her life. Someone who made you feel complete. To let you realize your true worth and value you for who you are.

"Let's have a party in the evening," Neha suggested. "We can celebrate Avni's achievement." Everyone was keen. Avni jumped with joy. She felt like her old self, the person who had been lost somewhere along the way, who was made to feel worthless by the man she had blindly fallen in love with, completely forgetting her true identity.

Everyone decided to go for a cruise down the Mandovi river in the evening. Vishal took responsibility of booking tickets for the cruise on Paradise, one of the Goa's biggest cruisers. The cruise took guests for a lovely ride down the river, past Adil Shah's summer palace towards the Arabian Sea and Reis Magos Fort. You could witness a panoramic view of the Grand Fort Aguada, majestic Cabo - the Governor's Palace, the sprawling Miramar beach and catch the glorious sunset over the vast Indian Ocean. She missed Vivan, but she was happy with her decision to come here.

The atmosphere on the boat was festive. Aakash felt a surge of exhilaration infusing into his body. He stole a glance at Avni. She looked lovely in her dress, a bright yellow flowing wrap-around skirt and halter top. Her smiling face was such a far cry from her aloof demeanour that she used to have in the earlier days. Everyone was enjoying themselves, away from the monotonous routine of conference activities. They clapped along with the beat of the music. Aakash was standing next to Avni. He had never seen her so cheerful. She was dancing and singing with the others. Then it was announced that there would be a round of dancing for the couples in the crowd. Neha promptly took the dance floor with her husband who had accompanied her on the trip. Before Avni knew it, Aakash was standing in front of her, offering her his hand. And to her surprise, she spontaneously extended her hand and followed him. Their eyes met. It seemed that the whole world had stopped. And then, without saying a word, they started dancing. His one hand was on her slim waist and the other holding her hand. They moved in complete rhythm, their every step coordinated, in sync with the music. It was as if they had known each other forever.

Aakash whispered, "You are looking beautiful Avni."

She looked at him and saw a raw tenderness in his eyes with a feeling of warmth. "Thank you, Aakash." Strangely, she found herself enjoying his attention. She was treading in the prohibited territory, a place that she had decided never to visit again, but she found it difficult to stop herself. Avni didn't know if she would be able to travel that path again, if she would be able to reciprocate Aakash's feelings, for she had no idea about her own feelings. Still, she was finding it difficult to resist him; the longing in his eyes was intoxicating, gradually making her oblivious of the promise that she had made to herself once upon a time.

The next day, early in the morning, Avni saw her mobile flashing. She looked at the screen. It was Aakash calling. Her heart started beating fast. After last night, she couldn't keep him away from her thoughts. She was not able to comprehend how he was becoming irresistible to her. Every promise that she had made to herself was falling flat. The way he made her feel was something sublime. It wasn't the first time she had been complimented for her beauty, but the sincerity in his voice was something she was not able to forget. She had a hard time falling asleep. An inner war went on between her heart and mind, with her mind trying to be logical and stopping her from following her heart.

"Do you want to go to the beach?" he asked. "I don't have any commitment at the conference today. I have checked with the others too, but no one has responded yet."

She found herself blushing. "Yeah sure, I don't have anything on either."

"Okay then, get ready in an hour. I will call a taxi."

And then he hung up, not realizing how his call had unsettled Avni. She was excited, but a little puzzled at herself too. She couldn't believe she said yes so quickly. She had called Sia the previous evening and was satisfied that Vivan was not missing her much. So she really wanted to go and see everything there was to see without feeling any guilt of leaving her son back home.

It was a beautiful day in Goa, a far cry from the cold and dreary winter of Delhi. They reached the Agonda beach in no time. It was a beautiful long pristine stretch of the sea, sand and waves. The breathtaking view was so invigorating, Avni thought. She looked as far as her eyes could go. The sky was merging into the sea somewhere at the horizon. Sitting next to her, Aakash was studying her, silently wondering if he was perhaps catching a glimpse of the girl who had been lost somewhere along the way but had now found her way back.

They were both sitting there for some time when Aakash asked if she wanted to go in the water. She looked at him. "I would love to. It's been ages."

He didn't expect her to agree, so hearing those words was like music to his ears. Life was worth living because of these moments that filled your heart with warmth and gave you a reason to hope.

"I'm scared of big waves, though." There was a sense of hesitation in her voice. "I hope it doesn't get rough."

"You shouldn't be scared, Avni," he said. "It should be okay. Let's get ready." He gestured at the changing room a few metres away from where they were sitting.

"Okay."

He changed quickly and was waiting for her when he saw her emerge from the changing room. She looked gorgeous in her black swimsuit. He couldn't believe that she was a mother. It was impossible not to admire her well-toned body. Avni felt a little awkward and shy in front of him, but she thanked the sunglasses for hiding her feelings.

The next moment, they were in knee-deep water. The sea was relatively calm. They surfed on the small waves for some time as they hit the shore. "I told you it would be fun," Aakash told her when he saw her enjoying herself.

"Honestly. I am having so much fun," she said. It wasn't long before a huge wave came and swept Avni off her feet. Before she could realize what was going on, she was thrown away off into the deep end. She could hardly see anything as a heap of sand brushed across her face. She was gasping for breath when she felt someone's hand on her shoulder pulling her out towards the shallow area. She opened her eyes with difficulty. Aakash was now holding her close to his chest. They stood silently, unmoved with no words exchanged. Then after feeling a little settled, she spoke, "I thought I was going to die."

"I wouldn't have let you go." He said as he tightened his embrace, "I am there for you....always."

He said the words so earnestly that for a moment, she forgot everything. What was left was the horizon of hope where promises meet reality. But then, do earth and sky ever really meet at the horizon? They just appear to meet, she thought to herself.

She lifted her chin. He was looking at her fondly, not wanting to let her go. She smiled the same enigmatic smile that had captivated his heart since he saw her for the first time. She then stepped back and in spite of him not wanting to, he released her from his embrace.

They returned to the hotel just after the lunch. Soon after, Neha called Avni. "It's our last night tonight, so we are planning to go to a nightclub in the evening. Do you want to come along?"

Avni wasn't so keen. "Hope it's okay with you guys if I don't join. I am too tired."

Neha didn't press her further. She then called Aakash. She was sure that he would undoubtedly agree to join them. To her surprise, Aakash didn't seem excited. He said he was not sure and will think about it.

In the evening when Avni came out of her room to the hotel lobby to find some information about the shopping areas around the city, she was surprised to find Aakash there. How could he be here? Hadn't he gone to the club? He looked equally surprised to see her. He walked towards her.

"Didn't you go with them?" she asked.

"I didn't feel like it," he said. "You didn't either."

"Oh no! I was tired after our morning trip to the beach" She smiled faintly.

"I can understand," he sympathized. "What you are going to have for dinner? I was just searching for a good place for food."

"I am too tired," she said. "Perhaps just room service."

"Why don't you join me? There is a very popular dhaba just next door. We can have dinner there."

How Avni always loved the food at these dhabas – fresh, full of aroma and rustic charm. She remembered how she would insist for it when she would go out with her family.

"That's a good idea. I love dhaba food."

"Okay then, let's go," Aakash said. Avni loved the spontaneity of it.

They walked towards the dhaba. It was a small but a vibrant-looking place. The atmosphere was lively with a radio playing local Goan songs. Avni suddenly felt rejuvenated. "It's good we decided to come here. Better than being at the club. I feel claustrophobic at those places."

Aakash didn't say that he was a regular at clubs. In fact, in a way, he liked it. It helped him to forget his lonely existence. The loud music drowned his pain. He wanted to forget himself, and the atmosphere at these places provided him with the perfect getaway.

They ordered some local Goan food. Aakash also ordered *feni*, a local, favourite drink. As they waited for the food, they talked about the hospital, her thesis work which was almost finishing and also about Vivan. Aakash noticed how Avni's eyes would light up with any mention of Vivan.

"Do you mind if I ask you something?" He looked at her.

She found herself replying spontaneously, "Not at all, Aakash."

"Why do you take things so personally? After all, they are just patients. And we should just have a professional relationship with them."

"Perhaps, I identify with some of their pain," she said. After a pause, she continued, "Of course, not with their illness, but with some of their personal experiences in life."

"Like?" He met her eyes.

"To not to be cared for. To be made to feel worthless. To not be seen. To be cheated by the person they love and trust."

She then sipped water from the glass, "I don't know why I am telling you this, but I have gone through all of that in my marriage."

There was complete silence after that. For a long time, none of them said anything. Avni was surprised with herself. Why did she need to share this with him? She had no idea, but in some way, she felt comfortable talking about her past with him. She wondered when that level of comfort had crept in between them in the past year.

Aakash finally the broke the silence, "I can understand." He then looked down, swirled the drink that he was having and then without raising his head, said, "I have witnessed a lot of things in my own family. My mother has been physically abused by my father for as long as I can remember. It's a shame that I have been living with. I hate going back home that lacks a wholesome atmosphere. I have no idea how she has coped with it over the years. Perhaps she didn't leave him because of me. She is a financially independent woman. She could have easily opted for divorce. And this is all…after a love marriage."

He took a deep breath. He said it all as quickly as he could. It was like ripping off a bandage really fast, to cause less pain. He was surprised with himself with the outpouring about things he couldn't share with anyone. After what appeared like a tornado, Aakash looked up. She was watching him calmly. A sense of peace washed over him. The sweat on his face cooled down. For the longest time, ever since he had gained awareness, he'd been living his life with this secret draped so heavily over his shoulders. He remembered the person he used to be, a cheerful boy who loved life, who believed in the magic called love. He still had no solution, no way out, but for just this moment, he was sitting opposite someone who perhaps understood.

They had both come from misery, she thought, and survived it. They had overcome the pain. Although they had walked on different paths, perhaps their quest was the same – love. And in spite of the promise to herself to never fall in love again, to her surprise, she found herself feeling attracted to him. She wondered if it had always been there, but was hidden under cover of her fear of getting hurt again.

Vivan was ecstatic to see Avni when she returned home. It was the first time she had left him for so long, and now he was not willing to leave her for even a second. He snuggled comfortably in her lap, basking in the warmth of his mother's love. Sia joked how he had forgotten about her almost instantly, not willing to even look at her anymore. She was glad to see her sister looking so happy after so many years. Avi had a healthy tan and was glowing. Little did Sia know that it was love that had also contributed to her cheerful demeanour. For the first time in her life, Avni did not express her feelings to Sia. After Samir's episode, it was the most challenging thing to make her family understand how she felt for Aakash. They, too, were right in being protective of her, not letting her fall for someone who could hurt her again.

As of now, she wanted to keep the relationship untouched, unjudged and unknown. How could she defend something when she was not sure about it herself yet? It was better to leave things in the hands of destiny rather than coming in its way.

After tucking Vivan in bed, she finished some of her pending work, payed utility bills online and checked her hospital schedule for next week. Sleep eluded her. She couldn't stop thinking about Aakash. She found herself engulfed in the flames of love yet again. The experience with Samir had ensured that she had become a stone. Aakash had somehow managed to melt that stone. She didn't know where it would lead her to, where it would end, but was sure hopeful of a better future.

Avni was a little late for the hospital in the morning as Vivan didn't want to let go of her, perhaps fearing that she would be gone for long again. As usual, Mrs Joseph came to her rescue, making it possible for her to leave. As she drove, she remembered that Mrs Joseph would be off for her annual two weeks leave soon. Sia was not going to be able to come to her aid either. She thought of asking her mother to come down to take care of Vivan. There was still a lot of space between them, slowly being filled with the passage of the time. The gap hadn't yet cemented and was still very delicate. She finally decided that she would apply for leave from the hospital.

Once she reached the hospital, Avni hurried to see a young couple who was waiting for her. They were among her thesis cases, but over the last year, after the HIV diagnosis of the wife during the routine antenatal stage, she became very close to her. Besides supporting them as a doctor, she had given them emotional support to tide over the storm. She was awed by the husband's decision to stand by his wife after knowing her HIV positive status, even when his family members advised him otherwise. This was almost nine months ago. At the time, even Aakash was a little skeptical about the continuation of the pregnancy. But Avni was yet to see such a loving and caring husband who went all the way to support his wife. Today was the first time Avni was going to see their baby, and she was ecstatic. When she entered the clinic, Aakash was already talking to them. "Sorry, I am a little late."

"No worries." He smiled as he gestured towards the couple. Tina, the wife, was holding a beautiful baby in her arms. "It's all because of you Dr Avni that we are sitting here today with our little bundle of joy." The father, Raj added, "We are thankful for your support."

"Thank you! But you know, it was all because of you," Avni said. "It's all because of your love that this could happen." She then took the baby in her arms. "He is negative for HIV," she said as she tenderly looked at the baby.

Aakash was quietly observing their interactions. How much he had learned from Avni. He never believed in love, he never believed that a stupid girl who had once argued with him for allowing this couple to have a normal sex life would teach him so much. He looked at the 'stupid girl' who was busy playing with the baby and felt a sense of warmth filling his body.

16

Avni was on leave from the hospital for the next two weeks. It had only been three days, but he missed her so much. For him, not being able to see Avni even for a day was like being separated from his own self. He was now losing his new-found serenity, the peace that had surrounded him ever since expressing his deepest secret to her on that night in Goa. After realizing that he couldn't live peacefully without seeing her, he decided to visit her. He dropped by at hers in the evening, unannounced, for the fear that she might stop him.

Avni opened the door with Vivan tagging along behind her. She looked at him, her eyes wide with surprise. He kept looking at her, soaking in her beauty quietly all the while.

"Is everything okay?" she asked as she took Vivan in her arms.

"Not really." He smiled and said, "Can I come in?"

"Oh sorry!" she said as she moved away from the door. "Come in please." She found her heart racing at the mere sight of him.

He followed her into the living room. The floor was littered with Lego blocks. "Oh! Wonderful!" He smiled, "Looks like you guys are having fun playing with these. My most favourite toy of childhood days!"

Avni smiled back as she lowered Vivan on the carpet, "You can join us."

"My pleasure." Aakash joined them.

Vivan had started to show a keen interest in Lego blocks. He seemed delighted to see Aakash joining them. Vivan slowly handed Avni the blocks from the box, and she started building a house with them. Aakash was silently observing them. It was so heart-warming to see the mother and son duo building together. Avni was trying to give the structure the shape of a house, but was unable to do so with the blocks falling repeatedly. "Can I help you?"

Avni looked at him and smiled. "Sure!"

Aakash smiled back as he took a block from Vivan's little hand and started to put it all together. In the next few minutes, he completed the house.

"Great!" Avni cheered happily, "This was exactly what we wanted, isn't it Vivan?" She then looked at Aakash, "Thanks for completing my home."

Aakash looked back at her and smiled, hanging onto her words dearly. How he would have loved to complete her home. Avni, Vivan and him.

Avni asked Aakash to stay for dinner, and he was more than happy to do so. He helped her lay the table. Vivan sat in his high chair, and they sat on his either side, facing each other. Avni fed Vivan his dinner consisting of porridge and boiled vegetables. For herself and Aakash, there wasn't much to eat, just chapatti and potato curry. But for Aakash, it was the most sumptuous dinner he had ever had, full of love, happiness and warmth. Vivan soon wanted to go to sleep after he finished his food. Avni excused herself as she went to put him to sleep. When she came back, she was surprised to find everything wrapped up in the kitchen. The table was cleared, dishes washed and dried. "You shouldn't have done that." Avni said, "Thanks so much!"

"No worries at all." He smiled.

"Would you like to have some tea?" she asked.

"Yes please, that'd be great," he said as he pulled a chair to sit.

Avni brought tea for them, and they sat down together, chatting like long lost friends. Avni noticed how keen Aakash was to hear about Vivan's milestones, a topic that she was never tired of discussing. They were still talking when, as if on impulse, Aakash took Avni's hand in his own. "I really admire the way you have reshaped your life without any support."

Avni, filled with emotion, didn't try to withdraw her hand from his. She looked at him and then looked away, "I have been fortunate in getting so much support. From my sister, Mrs Joseph, Dr Neha, my colleagues, you... you all have supported me in this journey, and that has kept me going."

"How can you be so hopeful and positive about everything despite all that happened with you?" He asked with a genuine inquisitiveness in his voice, as if he wanted to learn to do the same.

"It isn't difficult either, if you ask me. The fact that we plan our days, weeks and months in advance shows that we, by nature, are perennially hopeful. We hope to wake up alive the next day, we hope not to die, we hope to live for so long, we hope and that's what keeps us alive. Hope has a lot of power; it helps you sail through the worst storms of life."

"Isn't there a sense of distrust that builds inside you? I have lost faith in relationships and marriages after looking at my parents' case. I consciously have stayed away from it all till now," Aakash persisted candidly.

"Where there is hope, there is no place for distrust." After a brief pause, she continued, "I still believe in the institution of marriage.... But perhaps it's not for me."

He was taken in by her voice that had a tinge of regret, perhaps a kind of acceptance of a harsh reality, And in that instant, he decided. He wasn't sure if it was the right moment for him to express his feelings for her. *But then, when did life give us the perfect moment? Sometimes we have to make a moment perfect.*

"You know Avni… I believe in destiny. I believe that we are destined to do the things that we would choose anyway. I don't know about your choices, I don't know what is destined for you, but I would choose you in a million lifetimes. For me, you are my destiny."

She didn't say anything and kept looking down at the floor for a while. But when she raised her head, he had a faint glimpse of a girl who was trying to believe again, believing that perhaps destiny was giving her another chance. Her eyes glistened with tears. She smiled closing her eyes, probably in a bid to provide those tears a release from the clutches of her past. She had no idea where destiny was taking her, but for the moment, she didn't want to come in its way.

For the next few days, Aakash was busy with some patients who were quite sick, and so he didn't have time to see Avni. As soon as he got time, he called her. Her voice reminded him of this unfamiliar longing he had never felt before. "What are you up to?" Without waiting for her response, he said, "I am going to see you after work." He hung up even before Avni had time to respond. She smiled to herself and felt a wave of unadulterated joy engulfing her. It had been so long, she thought. The void that had formed in her life for as long she could remember seemed to have been filled up with Aakash's love. The years of pain were melting away and all of a sudden, the horizon was visible so clearly. And somewhere there, the earth and sky indeed seemed to be meeting.

Vivan was fast asleep. As Avni waited for Aakash to come by, she left the front door open and started preparing coffee, his favourite cappuccino. She wondered why she wanted to do it. Was it love? No sooner had she switched on the kettle, she heard someone's footsteps. Before she could turn, he was standing behind her. He softly brushed aside her hair and kissed her on the side of her neck. All of a sudden, she felt so wanted, so loved. She turned and looked into his eyes. But the next moment, as if recovering from an electric shock, she stepped back. She looked away and then with much effort, looked at him.

"Aakash, can you handle the mess that I am in? Will you be able to understand my insecurities, my fears, my lack of trust, and my eccentricities? To live with the broken parts of me that can probably never be whole again? And share the darkness that engulfs my life every time my past takes over me?" He kept standing there, unmoved, unblinking, looking at her. "I don't know why I am falling in love with you; you deserve someone better who is not defined by her past, who doesn't have the baggage of her mistakes." She looked up. He was still listening to every word that was being said, imbibing every emotion they carried, and also understanding the things that were left unsaid. Tears had started falling from her eyes. He took her hands in his own, wiped her tears and offered her a chair to sit. He sat in front of her and spoke with his hands cupping her face.

"You know Avni… I have not fallen in love with you in an instant. Have you ever thought why it took me so long to express my feelings? I was attracted to you when I saw you for the first time. But I waited. I waited to understand the unsure girl, to know about her insecurities, to fathom her brokenness, to absorb her pain, to appreciate her dreams. I couldn't love you in pieces. I had to love you as a whole. If I am only going to love the parts that are beautiful and not the parts that are damaged, the parts that need healing, the parts that need sunshine, how could I ever love you? That can't be love. I want to love you in all your rawness, in your happiness, and in your sadness. And although I only found you in this life, it seems I have loved you forever."

Avni was looking at him, unable to believe what she was hearing. Suddenly all the years of apathy and indifference were melting away. She smiled through her tears, thanking him. Aakash offered her a glass of water as he removed strands of hair from her face. He then spoke again as he stood holding her hand, "And since when did you think that only you are broken? Have I not told you about my life? Am I not broken too? Can't two broken pieces join together to form a whole?" He paused as he wiped his own eyes. "I need you, Avni. We will be whole together. I promise you that I'll always be there for you, in brightness and in darkness."

For a few moments, none of them spoke. They kept looking at each other. But then he couldn't stop himself, and in the next minute, his mouth was on hers. She didn't resist. It was like years of pain and darkness suddenly evaporating in that one moment of eternity. She kissed him back. He held her with a passion that was unknown to her. Avni didn't realize how long she was in his embrace. It was the sound of boiling water in the kettle that finally broke the trance. Avni stepped back and looked at him. She then uttered something in a soft voice, something that he had been waiting to hear forever. "I love you, Aakash!"

On the way back home that evening, Aakash felt as if his search was finally over. He had found love of that one person he was seeking in every lifetime since eternity. He smiled to himself when he suddenly realized the meaning of both of their names. Avni meant the earth and Aakash meant the sky – their names signifying their union at the horizon, and beyond.

For Aakash, life had indeed changed. He was surprised with himself. He was smiling at small, inconsequential things, things that would usually make him frown. He stopped being arrogant, an attitude he had acquired over the years. His colleagues were amazed to see such a change in him. They had yet to discover the real reason, the story behind the transformation from the bad guy to a good guy. Neha was so happy to rediscover her long lost friend. She wondered if it was because of Avni, but she waited for him to tell her, rather than inquiring about it.

At home, Aakash's mother was equally surprised to find him so cheerful. He had stopped going to the nightclubs she hated and would sit with her for hours and chat happily. She noticed, however, that he avoided talking about Priya. At times she would try bringing up her name deliberately in conversation, but Aakash would diplomatically change the topic. She didn't like it, but was careful enough not to upset him by pestering him. For now, she was happy to have her son back, who had been lost somewhere in the maze of life. She was hopeful that one day, her dream would materialize and Aakash would agree to marry Priya.

And for Avni, life gave her a reason to be happy, to be her old self again. Aakash had now become a regular visitor at her home. Besides Avni, little Vivan and Mrs Joseph too waited for his evening or weekend visits. Mrs Joseph was happy to see how Avni was finally living for herself again.

❖

It was Sunday evening. Mrs Joseph had gone out with Vivan for the usual evening stroll. These days Vivan was getting quite hyperactive. He hated having to stay indoors in the evening and would force Avni to let him out with Mrs Joseph. Avni generally utilized this time to cook dinner. It gave Mrs Joseph a little break from kitchen duty. She had just started making some roasted vegetables when she heard the doorbell. It must be Vivan and Mrs Joseph. She must have forgotten something. Instead, she found Aakash, smiling widely at the door. She looked at him in surprise, "Weren't you supposed to be going to one of your friend's party?"

"Are you going to let me in or just quiz me right here?" He questioned with a cheeky smile.

As soon as he stepped inside, he pulled her close and kissed her on the lips. "I hate going to these parties now." He took a strand of her hair and started playing with it, "I just want to spend time with you. You make me feel so good that I don't need any of those noisy parties to fill the empty space that I felt all my life." He then looked deep into her eyes, "Ever since you came into my life, I feel so full and content. With you, it's all so simple, so free-flowing; it allows me to be me."

She looked at him, "I cherish your company. I love being loved, but you could have anyone you want in the world. Why me?"

He looked back and smiled, "But why would I want anyone else in the world?" He kissed her again, "I just want you."

"But there must be some reason." Somehow, today, Avni really wanted to know his feelings, to understand their relationship to be able to live without any fear. As they say, once bitten, twice shy.

She was not ready to go through heartbreak once again, another cycle of hurt and misery. "Why do you like me so much?"

Aakash was a little taken aback by the uncertainty, the feeling of insecurity in her voice. Here he was, leaving the whole world behind to be with her, and she still had doubts. But next moment, he understood. He realized that her wounds from her earlier relationship had yet not healed. "You want to know why I like you?" She stood there. Still. "There is no reason. And there should not be any reason. You can't love someone for a particular reason because the reason can cease to exist, can fade, can just disappear. Then what is one supposed to do? Stop loving that person?"

He took her hand. "I love you without any reason. I love you for who you are."

She hugged him. No words were enough to express what she was feeling. What a relief it was to not have to prove her worth to him. To feel like she was enough and didn't need any reason for it. She wanted to melt in his arms, to disappear in his vastness and become one with him. Aakash could feel the warmth of her body. They remained entwined for a long time before Aakash pulled her onto the couch.

They kept looking into each other's eyes where there was an ache, a yearning, a longing for the other. He could hear her rapid, shallow breathing which matched his own. He started showering her with kisses on her face and neck. He had never felt such an urge in his life. He wanted to make love to her now, to become a part of her, to merge with her for eternity. Her face mirrored his desires. She appeared to be waiting for him to love her, to own her, to complete her. He could feel himself getting aroused as he kissed her breast. But he didn't go any further, and just kissed her on the head before he stopped. She looked at him in surprise. Her eyes had a million questions which couldn't be conveyed through words, but Aakash had no answers for them. He knew why he chose not to go ahead, why he decided to wait, but he found it difficult to explain it to her. *Who would not like to make love to you Avni, but you are not one of those random girls that I fancy and forget about. You are unique, very special. I want our love to be a celebration. I want to be one with your soul before becoming one with your body.* Avni, as if reading his mind, understood. She has swept away in a wave of desire, and it was right on Aakash's part that he didn't take advantage of her. He kissed her on the forehead and left for a family dinner.

17

The next morning, enveloped in the fragrance of blooming love, Avni walked inside the hospital building. She had a busy day today and wanted to start the day early. She had barely stepped her foot inside the common room when she heard someone talking. It was Nikhil and Sanjay. She was about to greet them when she heard something which made her stop completely. "Aakash is having a good time with Avni. He is certainly fooling around, and that stupid girl is taking it all seriously." Sanjay said, closely followed by Nikhil's voice, "He has safely tucked his girlfriend, Priya away in London. I heard that both their families are quite keen to on them getting married." To which Sanjay replied, "A bit of time pass before marriage, it seems."

She froze. She stopped feeling her existence. It was all blank for the longest time before she slowly regained her composure. Then there was disbelief, denial, and anger; all happening in quick succession. Only to be followed by the familiar, gnawing, bitter feeling of betrayal. How it had come to haunt her again, the deception which was slowly trying to diminish her capacity to ever believe again. How she had wanted to defy it, but how could you defy your destiny, she thought. It was lurking somewhere in the corner, ready to attack her once again when she was truly happy in the relationship. The wound was the same. Just the perpetrator had a different name. It was all so familiar.

However much she tried, she couldn't shake off the familiarity; the pain was same but somehow more intense and penetrating; perhaps because of the scar of an old wound that was still raw. Avni couldn't stand there any longer and turned back. She walked back to the parking lot with slow steps, trying to absorb every word she had overheard, so they could confirm her unforgiving fate – that what was now broken inside her could never be repaired.

Avni started driving back home. It was an overcast sky, covered with dark shadows of clouds like her heart, but she pulled out her sunglasses from her handbag. It made the sky much darker, but it did manage to hide the tears that were not under her control anymore. *After all, love was not destined for her; how fallible we are as humans, not learning from our mistakes and keep hoping against hope.*

Vivan was ecstatic to see her back home so early, utterly unaware of what his mother was going through. *Ah! The perks of childhood, innocence was such a blessing.* Avni took him in her arms, ran to her room, closed the door and embraced him tightly. It was like his embrace would help her release the pain, the heaviness that her heart was feeling. She didn't know how long she wept, realizing only when she noticed Vivan's dress drenched with her tears. Baffled, Vivan kept looking at her for a while before trying to wipe away her tears with his small hands. It was then, it suddenly drew upon her that she could not afford to let him down. Avni took his little hand to her lips and kissed. Silently, she promised to herself that he would not pay for her mistakes and raw courage was born in her broken heart. She decided that she would grieve for her fate and accept it in all its entirety, but she would not grieve for her loss. *Perhaps she was blind all the time; Aakash was always like this, but she didn't see it, or rather, she chose not to see it. You can't lose what was never yours, to begin with.*

Avni knew it would take time to get over the pain, but she also knew that she would be able to overcome it, for she owed that to her son. But at the same time, she felt so incredibly lonely in the entire world, with no one except Vivan standing with her. Mrs Joseph was a little perturbed by her early return from work, but true to herself, she didn't prod much after Avni told her that she was feeling unwell and handed over Vivan to her. After lying down on her bed in utter silence, unwittingly her thoughts started pounding her head. She faintly remembered meeting Priya once at the cafeteria with Aakash. He had very conveniently introduced her as his family friend, she snickered. Even in those fleeting moments, she remembered her face clearly. Undoubtedly, Priya was elegance and charm personified. She thought of calling Aakash and asking him if it was true. But again, the uncanny resemblance to what had happened with Samir stopped her.

Familiar pain is worse than an unfamiliar one for you are aware of the grief it causes. She didn't want to go through that cycle of interrogation and confession or denial again. Only two things could happen, either he would accept it or deny it. For her, it wouldn't make a difference. The trust was gone. Her pain would be the same, whether he did it or didn't. She was not going to be able to believe him ever again. Avni remembered how Sia had always warned her. Sia always thought that some girls had a particular affinity for bad boys; they fell for the wrong ones. And that her sister was one of them. Perhaps, Sia had been right all along. She found herself relieved at the thought that her parents still had no idea about Aakash. She wondered how they would have taken all this, especially when things were just beginning to get better with them.

Mrs Joseph came in with a cup of coffee. She could see tear stains on Avni's face, but decided not to ask her anything. Pain needs to be felt to be able to be free from it. Avni started sipping from the cup when suddenly a deluge of emotions struck her.

All the resolves she had made to herself moments ago came crashing down. Suddenly her strength gave way to the feeling of unending emptiness; she wondered if she could ever forget Aakash, if she could ever blank him out from her memories. And then she cried. She cried for lost love. She cried for being wronged. She cried for being not able to undo her past. She cried for the mistake that she had not committed. Yes, loving Aakash was not a mistake, unlike it was with Samir. It was not an impulsive feeling, but a slow, gradual falling in love. It was a decision of a lifetime and not a random act of infatuation.

It was late in the evening when Aakash called. Avni's first reaction was not to pick up the phone, but on second thoughts, she decided to. It was better to end things as quickly as possible, rather than carry the pain of inevitable hope mixed with hopelessness for too long.

"Yes?" Her low but firm voice surprised Aakash.

"Is everything okay?" he asked, "You sound low."

"You shouldn't have lied to me." She tried to hold back her tears. She was determined to finish the matter now, and she continued without waiting for a response. "Why did you mess around with me when you and Priya were already in a relationship?"

"I am sorry, but what's this about?" Aakash was now shocked. But before he could say anything else, further onslaught followed. "And don't be sorry. I trusted you, so it's my fault, not yours."

He heard her suppressed cry when she said, "Well, anyway, best wishes to you and Priya."

And the line went dead.

Aakash had never been so flabbergasted in his life. This was way beyond his imagination. She should have at least asked him if all that was true before concluding things. He was at least entitled to explain, to defend himself. What kind of judgment was this where there was no hearing? But somewhere inside, he knew. He knew that the bravest thing she had ever done was to love again, to believe again. It was not easy for her to trust someone again. He had done as much as he could to reassure her, but he could understand her insecurities.

Aakash reflected that it was futile to call her again, at least for now. He had seen how fierce and tender she was, within the same breath; it was that one thing that had always intrigued him. He had also seen the total lack of both; she was utterly indifferent. She loved deeply. With everything she had, or not at all. He then slowly reached for the cabinet and poured himself a glass of wine. A million thoughts crossed his mind. How did this happen? Who told her? He was unsure of many things, but he was sure of one, that his love was forever, unconditional as he had fallen for her soul.

That night was one of the worst nights in Avni's life. Tears just refused to stop flowing. She had reached a stage where she was barely able to breathe. She felt as if she would choke up and die. The heaviness in her heart was pulling her down, and she had crumbled beneath its weight. Aakash had shown her how vulnerable she was.

Pain demands acceptance. It wants to be felt, experienced and lived. The more you try to run away from it, the more it grabs you tightly in its clutches. But the moment you acknowledge it, the redemption starts. Accept it, and you heal. Escape from it, and it hurts you more. Perhaps it's god's way of asking us to cry it out and be done with it. Avni had learned this the hard way.

18

The next morning, Aakash woke up feeling a little better. There was hope. You never lose hope when you're hopelessly in love. There was a certainty that Avni would never leave him, he would make her understand everything and explain in detail about Priya and about his mother's obsession with her. He wondered if he should have told her all this before. But how could he have known that things would take the wrong course? He instantly dialled Avni's number and waited for her to answer. Her anger must have evaporated by now. Even if it hadn't, he was happy to be at the receiving end of her wrath. To love is to accept the person as a whole, with all of one's positives and negatives, in good and bad, in happiness and sadness. There was no reply. *She must be busy. I will find her and talk to her; she was never too far away.*

But she was. She had gone too far in a matter of a few hours. When she got up in the morning, she decided to not to let herself down anymore. She had to move on, without Aakash. For a moment, his name again elicited the agonizing pain in her heart that had overpowered her since the previous morning, but this time she didn't let it overwhelm her. Instantly she tried to take control of herself. First off, she blocked his number. She had no intention of making any further meaningless conversation with him. She also decided to request Dr Kapoor to change her unit. She would come up with an excuse, she thought. At least it would minimize interactions with him. During meetings and seminars, she could easily act professionally towards him. Her old armour, the shield of indifference would again be put in place.

She might have not been successful in beating her destiny, but she could always beat its consequences, she thought. She carefully selected her outfit for today, a bright yellow sari to counter the darkness she was feeling inside her heart. She took the time to do her make-up. Her swollen eyelids from a night of crying needed a little extra eye-liner and mascara to hide. She didn't want anyone to guess what she was feeling. Her pain was hers only, a precious treasure not to be shared with anyone. It would also make things look seemingly normal, the way she wanted. As far as Aakash was concerned, she had no idea how she was going to avoid him, but she was sure she would be able to.

She walked towards the office of the HOD, Dr Kapoor who was about to leave for the morning rounds shortly, but agreed to see her before that

"Sir, this is regarding my posting," she said keeping her face straight. "I would like to work in the ICU for a few months, as I was not able to do earlier because of my infant son. You would agree, that I must have the experience before finishing up my post-graduate degree."

She knew that she couldn't ask for any other change. Because of Vivan, she had repeatedly excused herself from the ICU posting, but now she had no choice. She decided that she would request her parents to come and stay with her for Vivan. She wondered how much had changed in a matter of a few hours. She was ready to do anything except go back to Aakash and ask him if what she had heard was true. She didn't know if she was wrong somewhere by not giving him a chance to explain things, but she knew one thing for sure, she didn't want to go through that cycle of pain yet again.

"Oh! That's a good decision. But are you sure you want it to do it now? Is your son stable enough? There is still a lot of time left to do that."

"I am sure sir!" There was a strange calmness in her voice.

"No worries!" he said as he rose from his chair to go for rounds. "I will discuss with the unit heads and see if we can post you there. My office will inform you of the decision soon."

"Thank you, sir!" She felt relieved. At least Dr Kapoor hadn't outrightly rejected her request. She was hopeful that it would be granted. Then, once her post-graduation was done in another six months, she could leave this place. A strange fear swamped her, the fear of being a coward and running away from the harsh realities of life. In the next instant, her mind justified that this was the need for survival, and if it meant cowardice, so be it. She knew she could never stop loving Aakash, but she could always make peace with the broken pieces of her heart by staying away from him.

After meeting Dr Kapoor, she requested for a two-day leave from her unit, which she was instantly granted. This would allow her to wait for the orders from the HOD for her posting in ICU, before resuming her work again. It was an absurd thing to do, but that was the only way to distance herself from Aakash. As planned, she went back home around lunch time after seeing a few urgent patients in the ward. Thankfully, Aakash wasn't around as he was on emergency duty for the day. Once home, she decided to tell Mrs Joseph honestly about what had happened between her and Aakash. She didn't want to face Aakash if he visited her at home. And it indeed was necessary as Aakash came around in the evening to see her as he couldn't get through to her on the phone the whole day, not realizing that it was all deliberate. How could he have ever imagined that the love of his life would want to stay away from him for the sake of the love they once shared?

Mrs Joseph emptily stared at Aakash and told him that Avni was not interested in seeing him. He wondered where all her warmth had vanished and turned to a future where nothing was ever going to be the same again. Perhaps he had never known the depth of his own love until this very moment of separation. For the first time in his life, his eyes were moist. *I am irreversibly changed by her, I can never unlove her.*

And then he slowly walked toward his car standing in the driveway. Avni caught a glimpse of him through the window, and her heart stopped for a moment. She could feel the gut-wrenching pain hitting her once again. Instantly she turned back. And suddenly, she couldn't understand whether talking to him hurts or not talking does. She slowly wiped away her tears and walked away to the backyard.

It was a quick decision. In fact, a long overdue posting was finally being put in place. An order was released from the office of the HOD that Avni would be posted in the ICU with immediate effect. For her, it was a victory and defeat at the same time. She had won against him, but she had lost against her own self. How easy it was to think that she could let go of him from her heart by being away from him and how difficult it was to actually do it. How can you let go of something that had become a part of your being? With much effort, she reached the unit on the first day of her duty.

She had to forget him and the environment here was perfect for her to get insanely busy with patients, leaving her with no time to think about him. But she was not so fortunate when she was at home, not working. It helped that her parents were here. After learning about her ICU posting, they couldn't stop themselves and moved in with her. They were worried about Vivan. It was a blessing in disguise; it helped them develop a cordial relationship. Now Aakash wouldn't visit her, and her parents would remain unaware of his existence. Sia, on the other hand, was a silent witness to the roller-coaster ride her sister was going through. The sudden changes in her behaviour didn't go unnoticed as Avni was bad at pretending, but the joy of having her parents back made up for it all.

Aakash didn't try to call her again. For Avni, it was a no-win situation. It had already been two months since they had last met. Although she had cut him off, whenever she got a phone call, she half-expected his name to flash on her phone screen. Perhaps it was merely out of habit, she tried to reason with herself.

Avni's hectic schedule left little time for anything else. With Vivan growing up, she was just shuttling between home and the hospital. Her parents were taking good care of Vivan, but Avni couldn't let go of her habit of satisfying herself with all the arrangements that were in place for him. Vivan would see very little of her and hence continually tail her when she was home. One of the days, after not being able to find Avni at the hospital, Dr Neha visited her at home. She knew about them. After initial formalities, she came directly to the issue that was concerning her. She was not known to discuss personal things, but today, she felt obliged for the sake of her friendship with them.

"Aakash met me when I was a mess," Avni said, "Perhaps that's why I got carried away. He took advantage of me."

"You know Avni, I am not speaking for him, but real love doesn't meet you at your best. It meets you in your mess."

Avni kept looking at her, not knowing if she could believe her. After a while though, she just mumbled in affirmation, but she knew that she could never tread that path again. But perhaps, until now, she hadn't really understood Aakash.

If Avni was trying to forget him by keeping herself insanely and at times unnecessarily busy, Aakash was trying to remember her in every possible way by finding her existence in every little thing, to forget his own existence in every way possible. She successfully avoided him at any departmental meetings by either not being there or not acknowledging his presence. She would just look through him if he tried to make any eye contact. He knew that she could do that. He had experienced it in the initial days when she had just joined the hospital. But he didn't know how difficult it was for her to do that now. How it was taking all her strength to unlove the person she was irrevocably in love with. How easy was it to fall in love, but how difficult to fall out of it!

He loved his work, and that was somehow keeping him sane, but he had resumed his drinking again. It was Avni who had introduced him to a newer self, and now it was Avni only who was forcing him to forget himself. It was like replacing one addiction with another. Drinking helped. He also tried to resume clubbing and partying, but somehow failed miserably. It was impossible. He would try to look for her face in every girl he encountered, try to find her in the crowd that she never belonged to.

She could keep herself away, but she could never be successful in erasing memories of their time together, he reflected as he poured another drink for himself. He didn't realize when he dozed off later, but the nightmare was back again. He found himself consumed by the same dark abyss that he had forgotten about after Avni had walked into his life.

His mother, Mrs Mehta was acutely observing this sudden change in her son. The constant smile on the face with a happiness that had become a distinct part of his existence off late had gone missing. He was going back to his old ways, mechanically living his life. She also noticed how his drinking had increased. The son she had found after ages was lost again somewhere. She called Priya to tell her that she should come back from London. Mrs Mehta believed that it was the right time for Priya to re-enter his life.

She had doubts regarding his relationship with Avni, but all her fears were laid to rest after listening to his response when she asked about Avni. Without taking his eyes off the laptop, he had answered that she had her own life and was busy with studies and her child. She had inwardly rejoiced at the fact that he sounded so distant, so aloof about her. She was sure that Priya would not only make him forget Avni, but would also establish an everlasting relationship with him. And her long-time dream of seeing them get married would be materialized. As it was, the very thought of him marrying a divorcee, and that too with a child, gave her shudders. She didn't even want to think of that possibility.

19

Aakash was absent-mindedly surfing through TV channels in the evening when Priya suddenly appeared in their family room. She had never lost the hope, and perhaps now it was time for those hopes to bloom into a million dreams. She had arrived from London a day back after she had got a call from Mrs Mehta. Everyone was perfectly playing cupid in uniting the two. Rajiv had arranged for a get-together at their home on the forthcoming weekend to once again celebrate his sister's homecoming and give them ample chance to clear misunderstandings of the past. He wanted to bring them closer so that he could broach the topic of marriage, this time with a definite answer. Dressed in a short black dress and matching stilettos, Priya was looking stunning. Her shoulder length, straight hair was shining brightly with not a strand out of place. She smiled radiantly when Aakash looked at her.

"Surprised?" she quipped.

"No," he replied. There was no change in his expression. "Just curious."

He then looked at his mother who was still standing there in the hallway, his expression as cold. "Aren't you supposed to be having your mid-semesters exams? Rajiv was mentioning that to me the other day."

Priya could feel the familiar feeling of being 'not wanted' gripping her, but she tried to stay calm. Mrs Mehta quietly left them alone.

"I have deferred it this time." She barely tried to keep her feelings in control; feelings that were a strange mix of love, anger, empathy, hope.

"I see." That was all he could mouth.

"Let's go out," Priya tried to sound chirpy. "We can have dinner at a new Japanese restaurant." Priya was speaking as though nothing unpleasant had ever happened between them and things were same as always.

"I can't," he said. His answer was as brief as his interest in her.

When she couldn't take it anymore, her patience completely wearing out, she suddenly asked, "Are you and Avni still together?'

He looked at her and then kept staring at her for a long time before looking away. *So, she knew. Well, 'how' wasn't important. She knew, and that was enough.* Collecting his thoughts, he signalled her to sit. That's when without blinking his eyes, he said, "You know Priya, the bond forged between me and Avni was not one that could be broken by absence, distance or time. As I would always belong to her, so would she always be mine."

That was coming from a man whom she had loved unceasingly, maybe from the day she had seen him for the first time. It was not only a declaration of his love for Avni, but also an affirmation of the truth that love could never be demanded or forced; it just existed or did not. It was also a confirmation that her hopes were truly and finally demolished, that she could still love him, but he was never going to love her back. It was a bitter revelation. Tears started rolling down her cheeks. It seemed there was nothing left in her. After a few moments, gathering what all was left in her, she looked up to find him standing there in the corner of the room, looking somewhere in the distance at the horizon with a glass of wine in his hand. She walked up to him, perhaps to say a final goodbye.

"I am sorry. I shouldn't have expected so much from you," Priya said. "I can understand your feelings, Aakash. Avni has no idea how fortunate she is." Her voice was strangely calm. Aakash turned to look at her. She smiled faintly and then waved goodbye as she left the room.

No sooner had Priya left their home that Mrs Mehta appeared on the door. Aakash was a little taken aback for a moment after finding her there again, but didn't say anything. He had done something that his mother wouldn't have approved, and he understood. He tried to diffuse the situation.

"Let's have dinner."

It was as if she didn't listen.

"Can I ask you a question?" she said. "I have been meaning to have this conversation with you for a long time, but now it seems imminent." Then she looked at him, an unmistakable shadow of hurt and disappointment covering her face.

"Mom, you don't need my permission." Sheepishly, he took her hand and made her sit, sitting down next to her.

"Do you realize what you are doing?" She threw bloodshot eyes on her son, "I know for whom you are rejecting Priya."

He remained silent. His head bent down, staring at the floor. After not getting any instant response, she continued, "Avni. I know all about her. A divorcee with a kid."

There was still no response from her son. She went ahead. "Who knows why she could not keep her marriage? What was the reason for her divorce? Whether it was she who was responsible for it? And anyway, why do you have to be involved with her? You are not supposed to take care of her." He looked up, and their eyes met. "I still can't fathom how you can leave Priya for such a woman."

Aakash kept looking at his mother for some time before he spoke, "I wish I didn't have to answer your question, but perhaps that's the only way I can make you understand."

"Mom, you kept your marriage intact, isn't it?" He looked away, trying to avoid any eye contact. "But at what cost? Were you ever happy? Could I ever have a normal upbringing? Weren't there enough reasons for you to divorce dad? In spite of everything, you had to suffer humiliation all your life." Then he looked at her, gathering enough courage to say what he was going to say, "But you never had the courage. And Avni precisely had that thing in her. She was brave enough to walk out of a bad marriage, where she was being cheated on by her husband. She preferred to live on her own. She preferred to give her son a better atmosphere. She preferred to not suffer silently. Now tell me, Mom, is there anything wrong in that?"

Mrs Mehta was speechless. Yes, this was what she could have done, but chose not to, and lived with shame all her life. Suddenly there was a realization of the undeniable truth that she was trying to hide from, all her life. Strangely, she didn't feel insulted. She just looked at Aakash with moist eyes and slowly nodded.

"Yes, I didn't have the courage. Avni certainly has."

"Mom, I am sorry if I hurt your feelings, but perhaps precisely for this reason, I admire her. I have seen her struggling to make her own place in the world. I admire her grit and determination. Her beauty, instead of being a boon was a bane to her, but she has elegantly managed to come out as a winner."

Mrs Mehta didn't say anything but she was inwardly feeling proud of her son for his understanding and depth of feelings. Possibly, it was his way of dealing with the unpleasant past that he had to endure, to fall in love with a woman who represented what his mother lacked – courage, determination, and high self-esteem.

"And Mom, as far as loving her is concerned, I must tell you that I am incapable of loving anyone else except Avni. She is my past, present and future, and no one can ever take that away from me, not even she, herself. " Aakash had finally managed to tell the unshakable truth before trying to get out of the unwanted situation.

She finally spoke, "I am sorry for letting you down … for not having enough courage, for not standing up for myself, for not really understanding what you must have gone through." She touched his hand, "But I know I still have a chance to undo at least some damage."

She then got up, kissed him on his forehead and said, "I have not known my son as well as I thought I did. I am proud of you."

Aakash also got up and hugged his mother. She hugged him back. Finally, she was able to reclaim her son whom she had lost in the maze of life.

"Hope I get to meet Avni soon," she said, knowing well that not all was going perfectly between them.

"Certainly Mom!" He looked into her eyes, "If I can see her again."

❖

Sia was ecstatic. She and Avni could finally have a long overdue outing together, an overseas trip to London. Avni had to go for an international conference. Sia also had some office related work in London. She coordinated it with Avni's travel plans so they could go together. Avni was leaving Vivan for the first time for an overseas trip, but she was reassured by her parents that she didn't need to worry about him. As it was, Vivan was almost inseparable from his grandparents. He adored them. And they doted on him. It was like they wanted to compensate for the lost time. Mr Trivedi had perhaps forgotten all about the painful past. Avni was so happy to see the change. It was as if she had been redeemed of all her sins. She felt relieved that they never got to know about Aakash. Her love story never blossomed as much to attract any thorn. Perhaps that would have created a permanent fissure in her relationship with her parents, never to be ever filled again.

As for Avni, an ache, a longing for Aakash never ceased to end, however much she tried. It was like being in labour; the pain could only get worse. How much she wanted to hate him, she couldn't go beyond the feeling of deep hurt something like a huge block of pain lodged in her heart. Sometimes when she was alone, she would feel Aakash around herself with his devastatingly attractive smile that would make her forget all her worries. In those moments, she really wanted to see him. It was such a wrong, weird desire that she refused to ever acknowledge it.

Perhaps for this very reason, to break the cycle of his painful memories, she chose to attend the conference in London. She wasn't sure if it would help, but at least she would live with the knowledge that she had tried. Sia was her cheerleader who was entirely of the opinion that Avni needed a break. And what could be more worthwhile than a trip to Europe in early April? She had cajoled Avni to add Amsterdam in their itinerary. She had heard a lot about beautiful tulips that grew there, particularly during this time of the year.

However much Avni reassured herself, she found it hard to be so far away from Vivan and that too, for so long. Two weeks was indeed a long time for her! But after constant reassurance from her parents, she felt a little better and started the preparation for a two-week long trip. Avni had her conference in London and Sia had her office work. After that, they intend to have one week stay at Amsterdam.

Their flight was at 1 a.m. Vivan and her parents came to see them off at the airport. Vivan was fast asleep in her father's arms by the time they reached Indira Gandhi International airport. As Avni kissed him goodbye in his sleep, she desperately tried to control her tears. It was like she was leaving behind a part of her soul, a precious possession and the only reason for her to live. Perhaps her mother could really understand her turmoil. She hugged Avni and reassured her once again. "Don't worry, it would be okay." Sia also immediately took Avni's hand in her own, "Mum and Dad are there. They have raised us as well. They know how to look after a child." But Avni knew it was never going to be easy for her. As they waved goodbyes to their parents and walked towards the departure lounge, Avni's intent gaze lingered on Vivan until the moment she stepped into the lounge and finally lost the sight of him.

Only after they reached their hotel in London, it finally occurred to Avni that she was here for her conference and had to be ready for that. It was already evening there, and her conference started the next morning. She needed to review her presentation and work on the finer details. A good diversion for her, Sia thought. She seriously needed some time-off from her hectic schedule, both from the hospital and the home. Sia had still not asked her much about Aakash though it was all apparent to her. She knew Avni well enough to know her innermost thoughts, but she wanted to give her time. Somehow she had a feeling that things hadn't shaped up the way they should have. An unmistakable emptiness in Avni's eyes invariably caught Sia's attention. She would miss her cheerful demeanour that could light up any room, which had appeared and disappeared with the arrival and departure of Aakash from her life. Not ever been in love herself, Sia at times wondered if it was worth it to lose yourself in search of someone else. Wasn't it that in the desire to be loved by someone else, we forget to love our own self? In the process of looking for an unquestioned commitment from other, weren't we betray our own selves? But whatever it was, she wanted her sister to be happy and was hopeful that this trip would help her to heal her wounds.

Avni was happy that her presentation went very well. There was a lot of curiosity about the management of people living with HIV in India, and she had quite successfully managed to answer the questions posed by the other delegates. It was the first time she was attending such a large scale international academic feast, and she found it a good learning experience. In spite of her not wanting to, her thought wandered off to Aakash. She remembered the great time they had in Goa, her first ever conference as a junior fellow, the time he had proposed to her officially. She wondered how it would have been if he had accompanied her here too. She found it surprising that thoughts like these still warmed up her heart. Perhaps she could never stop loving Aakash. She could only withdraw herself from his life by creating an impenetrable shield around her. She didn't have any other option. On the way back, from the Convention centre to her hostel on famous London tube, a loved-up couple lost in their own world was sitting just across Avni. Unknowingly, she stared at them a little longer than usual as if to finally realize that this kind of love was not destined for her. She took a deep breath and shifted her gaze outside.

Sia took care that whatever time they could spare from their work schedules was spent in sight-seeing and shopping. She took it upon herself to book tickets for various tourist attractions in London. She was happy to see Avni enjoying the much-needed break. They shopped a lot. Vivan, as usual, was at the top of their list. If Avni could, she would have perhaps bought truckloads of things for him. It was never enough for him. They also bought stuff for their parents, in spite of being told every day on Skype to not to do so. Skype sessions in the evening ensured that Avni got to see Vivan every day. Although at times, she felt a little pang of jealousy that Vivan would remain distracted during those times, paying more attention to his grandparents and didn't seem to be missing Avni much. But at the same time, she was happy that he was not missing her.

Their time in London passed very quickly. Now it was time for Amsterdam, a week of pure fun. No conference, meetings or work. They were having dinner in the hotel which they had earlier ordered through the room service. Today was their last day in London, and they wanted to go to bed a little earlier than usual. Their ongoing flight to Amsterdam was early next morning. Sia had switched on the television. Suddenly news flashed in red: **Major air-traffic disruption across Europe due to ash-cloud**. It was followed by the report. "The ash cloud produced by the eruption of a sub-glacial volcano in Iceland has caused closure of majority airports in Europe. A very high proportion of flights within, to, and from Europe are being cancelled."

"What?" Sia's face contorted, "What the hell is going on?"

Avni looked at her in disbelief. "This is insane."

"Ok!" Sia sighed, "Let me call British Airways." Avni kept staring at the TV screen, completely forgetting about the food. After being kept on hold for some time, she could get through the operator who confirmed what they had just heard. Their flight to Amsterdam was indeed cancelled, and there was no further information about the flight schedules.

"After ages, we could plan such a trip and see how it's turning out to be!" Sia exclaimed.

"It's okay Sia." Avni behaving like an elder sister, tried to sound calm, "It could have been much worse. We can always stay here in London till any further news." She smiled. "We can use our time here to do all those things which we couldn't do earlier."

"You have changed so much!" Her eyes held Avni's as she spoke, "You would have reacted so differently a few years back. You accept whatever situation you are in and try to look at the positive side."

"Life teaches you, Sia… a lot." Avni said reflectively.

Sia couldn't have agreed anymore. She had witnessed Avni's transformation more than anyone else.

20

It was around midnight when Mrs Trivedi heard Vivan's cry. She wondered what it might be. He had slept after having a little fruit yogurt for dinner. He had a couple of loose motions during the daytime, and didn't seem much interested in eating anything. Mr Trivedi had told her not to force feed him and to let him have something light for dinner.

She tiptoed to his cot. The mild cry had now turned into a scream. He was curling up in bed in pain. Mr Trivedi also woke up after hearing the noise. Both tried to console him, but to no avail. He kept crying for a few minutes and then seemed like trying to sleep again. Mrs Trivedi caressed his head. But after a minute's gap, the crying started again. She took him in her arms, but he was irritable; not settling down in her arms. Then still, he was okay for a while before the pain started again. "It must be colic," she said to her husband.

By this time, Mrs Joseph had also come rushing to the room. "Oh no!" she exclaimed, "He used to have it when he was small. But he hasn't had it for a long time now." Meanwhile, the intensity of his pain seemed to have gotten worse. He was disconsolate. Mrs Joseph ran to the medicine cabinet and searched for the colic medicine Avni used to give him. She found it soon enough and ran back to the room.

After Mrs Trivedi gave him the drops, he rocked Vivan in his arms to make him sleep. But he wasn't successful. Vivan's crying increased as time passed by. And then he vomited. It was already more than two hours since the pain had started. They now started getting worried. "Should we call Avni?" Mrs Trivedi said. She waited for her husband's response as she cradled Vivan in her arms.

He paused for a few seconds before speaking, "We can take care of Vivan. That's why we are here." He looked at his wife, "And anyway, they are already worried about the ash cloud and their flight for Amsterdam being cancelled. Let's not bother her for now."

Mrs Trivedi felt pleasantly surprised by this change in his attitude. He was now the same loving, caring father who had once almost disowned Avni.

But even before both of them could think of anything else, Mrs Joseph suddenly interjected. It was like she had remembered something and now she had the solution. "I have his number," she said turning to get her diary.

"Whose number?" Mr Trivedi exclaimed, a little perturbed by her sudden suggestion. "The doctor's number who used to see him when he was small." She paused, knowing that she might be not doing the right thing and that Avni would be upset, but then she decided that this was not the time to think about those things. Whatever she was doing was in the best interest of Vivan.

"Dr Aakash!" And then she ran towards her room to get that old phone diary that still had Dr Aakash's name and phone number in its pages. During those good times when Avni and Dr Aakash were together, Avni had asked her to keep his number in case of an emergency, in case she was not reachable, and Vivan needed any immediate help. Mrs Joseph never required to use that number, but perhaps today was that day when Vivan really needed him.

Mrs Joseph was back with the diary. She opened the page where Dr Aakash's name and number were written. Mr Trivedi looked at her, "Who is he?"

Mrs Joseph had expected the question. She was ready with the reply that was not going to raise any issue, touch any dark areas or disturb any harmony. It was going to be as professional and as bland as it could be. She cared for Avni too much.

"He is Dr Avni's senior at the hospital." Her face was expressionless. "He once came to see Vivan when he had a similar kind of pain."

Either it was the delicacy of the situation or his changed behaviour, but he didn't ask anything further. "Okay," he said, "Please call him." He then turned towards his wife, "Hope he doesn't mind it."

Mrs Joseph instantly punched the number on her favourite old Nokia phone and waited for him to answer her call.

Dr Aakash, after finishing his gruelling twenty-four hours casualty duty at the hospital was finally home, just in time for dinner, much to the delight of his mother. Lately, the bond between mother and son had got a new life. Aakash would mostly be home after work, and they were once again connecting as a family. Dr Ramesh, the senior Mehta was also quite surprised with his son's regular presence at home. He did check with Mrs Mehta about the change, whether Aakash was still dating Priya (According to him the character called Avni was non-existent in Aakash's life), but got an ambiguous response from her.

Nevertheless, he liked the change. It was good to see Aakash spending time at home.

After dinner, Aakash went to his bedroom. He was tired, but sleep eluded him. It was nothing new; Avni had ensured that. Her enduring presence all around him wouldn't let him. It was like time had paused ever since she had made that last phone call that ended all his dreams. Since that moment, he hadn't moved a bit while the world around him had perhaps gone very far. He would just lay awake for the longest time every night, thinking what it could be if not for the painful misunderstanding, till the time sleep showed mercy on him by enveloping him in its arms. However much he reasoned, he could never find any fault in her. She did what anybody would have done in her situation. She couldn't afford to be deceived again. It was entirely his fault. He should have told her all about Priya. He shouldn't have kept anything hidden from her. *To love is to be honest, nakedly honest.*

Aakash was still in deep thoughts when he suddenly found his phone ringing. *No, now don't tell me there is an emergency at the hospital and no one else can handle it.* He thought to himself warily as he picked up the phone from the bedside table. He looked at the name. Next moment her old, wrinkly but adorable face flashed before his eyes. Mrs Joseph. He wondered why he still had her number on his phone. At first, he thought that she must have pressed it by mistake and decided to let it go. But when there was a second call again, he decided to answer it.

"Hello! How are you, Mrs Joseph?" he said.

Mrs Joseph was relieved that he recognized her instantly. It was as if the intervening period never happened, like he was still seeing Avni, still coming to their home and playing with Vivan. It was hard to tell why, but she always wanted them to be together.

"Sorry to bother you at this time, Dr Aakash!"

"No worries!" he said, his mind racing to find the reason for her call. He knew for sure that Avni was not in the city, having gone for the international conference. "Hope everything is okay, Mrs Joseph."

"Dr Aakash, Vivan. You remember Vivan?" she started saying.

"Of course, Mrs Joseph!" he said. "How could you ever think that I can forget him?" He felt a tinge of worry overcoming him, "What happened to him? Is he okay?"

"The thing is, he is crying inconsolably." She said, "You remember how he used to have those colic pain attacks when he was younger. He is actually having one of those, but this time, it's just not going." She gave a very apt description, Aakash thought.

"Any vomiting?" he asked

"Yes." She said, "Twice."

"Have you given any medicine?"

"Yes, the same one that Dr Avni used to give him."

"Have you called Dr Avni?" he asked. The formality in his tone, adding 'Dr' to her name didn't go unnoticed by Mrs Joseph, but she replied in a matter of fact tone, "Not yet."

"Are you alone with him?" he asked, now fully alert, ready to don his doctor's gear. But before that, he just wanted to be sure about the situation at Avni's home. It was an odd situation, to say the least. He was supposed to attend Vivan in Avni's absence, someone who had wholly deleted him from their lives. And he doubted if she was ever going to see him again.

"No… Dr Avni's parents are here," she said, promptly adding, "They stay with us now." Probably she also wanted to make him aware of about the new circumstances there. For a moment, Aakash hesitated. He wanted to ask if Avni's parents were aware of his existence and about what he and Avni shared in not much distant past. *But wasn't that all irrelevant? Wasn't he just supposed to do his duty as a doctor?*

"Okay!" His professional tone was well in place, "I will be there soon."

On being briefed about the developments, Mr and Mrs heaved a sigh of relief and thanked Mrs Joseph.

It was 3 a.m. when Aakash reached Avni's home. It took him less than fifteen minutes. *How could he not find his way easily*! He remembered every street, every road that leads to Avni's home by heart. Nothing had changed, except the distance between them, an infinite distance that nothing could fill in, except perhaps the destiny.

It was Mrs Joseph who immediately opened the door as soon as he pressed the call-bell. She hurriedly directed him to Vivan's room, while Mr and Mrs Trivedi looked at him, his serious, intense look impressing them instantly. He wished them before asking Mrs Trivedi to put Vivan on the bed. He looked at him. He was all sweaty, restless and crying incessantly. He started examining him. He checked his vitals and then he palpated his abdomen as gently as possible. There was a visible sausage shaped abdominal mass. At once, Aakash knew that it was a case of small intestine obstruction. He suspected intussusception but refrained from saying anything at this stage. He was not a specialist pediatrician. An X-ray or CT scan was still needed to be done to confirm the diagnosis. He checked for the signs of dehydration, generally seen in these cases and found them. His skin was looking less elastic, and anterior fontanel (soft spot on the head) was sunken. He checked about the frequency of urine from Mrs Trivedi. She told that he was not wetting his diaper as often. Aakash knew it was an emergency. Vivan was going into shock, a worrying symptom for such a small baby. Even before explaining anything to the Trivedis, he called the hospital and asked for an ambulance.

"We need to admit him." He told them once he was done with arranging the ambulance in a thoroughly professional tone. No signs of any shared history with their daughter. No signs of discomfort that such history might have bought.

Mr Trivedi looked at him, grateful to him for his promptness and no-nonsense attitude. "Thank you, doctor!" He said, "You are doing a great favour to us."

"Of course not, sir!" He said looking at Vivan's face, "It's my duty." He looked pale and floppy. Vivan was lying listlessly on the cot. It was as if he was trying to catch his breath before being caught by yet another wave of pain. For a split second, he looked back at Aakash. Although it had been more than six months since Aakash had last seen him, he felt as if he saw a faint glint of recognition in Vivan's eyes. His heart suddenly warmed up. He remembered how much he used to love spending time with him. Vivan would be so glad to see him. Avni told him so many times that Vivan would guess that he was on the door and excitedly wait for the door to be opened.

"Should we tell Avni?" Suddenly he heard Mrs Trivedi. He looked up. Her anxiety-ridden face was looking for an answer that he didn't have. As far as managing the case was concerned, he knew he could get the best possible treatment for Vivan. But he had no idea how Avni was going to react to his presence. For him, Vivan's health was more important than their shared past.

"If you wish so, but we can take care of Vivan." He tried his best to be ambiguous. "And also, I heard some news about an ash cloud over Europe and flights getting canceled in the evening."

"Hmm… let's wait," Mr Trivedi said with a concerned look in his eyes, "We can tell her once Vivan has stabilized."

"She would go mad if she gets to know about Vivan and won't be able to fly back," Mrs Trivedi said, nodding her head in agreement with her husband.

Outside, the sound of an ambulance approaching them got louder. Aakash instantly picked Vivan in his arm and proceeded towards the door, followed by Mr and Mrs Trivedi.

The ambulance was racing through the city streets towards the hospital. The IV line had been started for Vivan. Aakash looked outside when his eyes fell on the auburn sky, painted by the morning sun.

Vivan was immediately attended at the emergency ward. After being reassured about his airway, breathing and circulation, Aakash frantically started looking for the paediatrician on call. Dr Ajay Tandon, his batch-mate, was on call that day. He promptly reached Vivan's bedside after attending a case who was admitted before. Dr Ajay urgently placed a nasogastric tube to decompress the obstruction from above. He gently explained to Mr and Mrs Trivedi who were helplessly finding their little grandchild being suddenly connected to so many tubes. "Vivan needs a nasogastric tube, which is passed up the nose, down the food pipe and into the stomach. This will drain off the stomach and bowel contents, and vent any air that has built up, which will make your child more comfortable."

They looked a little relieved with the information. Still, an unmistakable fear filled the deepening lines on their faces. Avni had to be informed soon, Mr Trivedi thought to himself. After all, she was the mother. Dr Ajay further advised to put Vivan nil orally and started him on antibiotics. In the meanwhile, Dr Chandra, head of paediatric surgery, also arrived. He checked on Vivan and ordered him to be transferred to Radiology division for an X-ray before planning any further treatment.

Aakash was standing there silently, watching over Vivan as treatment strategies were being discussed. He was hopeful that Vivan just needed conservative treatment, the pneumatic reduction, and not any surgery. It must be the first time in life that he was so anxious. He prided himself to be a thoroughly professional, but today he was not able to identify himself with that person. It was as if he was experiencing Vivan's pain, feeling his agony, for he was not only a doctor today but also a keeper, custodian of a child whose mother was not by his side, and whose grandparents had trusted him with his life. It was still not so hot in Delhi, but he felt beads of sweat covering his forehead.

Suddenly he heard Mr Trivedi calling his name, "Dr Aakash!" He looked up. "It's Avni on the line." He said as he handed him, his cell phone. "We just talked to her. I told her not to worry as Vivan is better now. But she insisted on knowing about the medical problem that he is having."

For a moment, Aakash was dumbfounded. He would be talking to Avni. How long it had been since he had heard her voice. He wondered what she would say. *Would she thank him? Would she forgive him? Or should he expect precisely the opposite? She would hate him more for entering her life, again…without her permission and approval.* He felt his heart racing. It was difficult for him to hold himself together. Avni however, made it all easy for him.

"Aakash here," he said. Barely managing to hide his apprehension, not letting his tone getting overwhelmed by what he was feeling.

"Thank you for your help, Dr Aakash!" He heard the familiar voice, but the coldness was unmistakable. She addressed him with the 'Dr' title, a deliberate act on her part. And he didn't miss it. Perhaps she wanted to remind him of the infinite distance that now existed between them. He knew her well. She didn't really need to make extra effort to address him so formally. Did he really even matter to her anymore? A thought suddenly hit him like an avalanche. Pain seeped through every pore of his existence. For a moment, it felt that he couldn't breathe. It was like being buried under piles of snow of memories of him and her together, of love, of loss. But then the pain was followed by the numbness. Suddenly there was nothing left, no feeling, no pain, nothing except that he was a doctor and was just discussing Vivan's condition with his mother. A truly professional person that he was, didn't allow his feelings to rule his mind at the moment.

"I am sorry for all the trouble." He heard her saying. "I wish I could fly back." Her voice quivered. She couldn't pretend anymore. Her heart was sinking with every passing moment. There was so much she wanted to share with him – her pain, and her anguish. But she didn't. She couldn't. It was not her Aakash anymore, who could take away every pain of hers, just by being there in her life. Now he was just a fellow colleague who was taking care of Vivan and helping her parents.

"No worries. I am here," he said, "Vivan is suspected to have intussusception. Further investigations are being done. We are waiting for the reports. Further treatment would depend on the reports."

Avni also then heard a quite familiar voice, a thoroughly professional one devoid of any emotions akin to what she had first encountered when she met him for the first time. She winced. How much she had avoided him since that day when her world had irreversibly changed, after she had got to know about him and Priya and how miserably she had failed all along. How difficult it was for her to not show how badly she missed him, how much she still loved him. Perhaps it was much easier to show love than to hide it.

"Can I talk to the paediatrician on call?" she said when she couldn't continue anymore. It was hard to be concerned and being indifferent at the same time. Vivan was too precious. Her past should not cast any shadow on him.

"Yes," he said knowing well that she was avoiding him, "Please hold on."

He then passed the phone to Ajay who explained Vivan's condition to Avni. She then requested to talk to Prof Chandra, who promptly obliged. Aakash kept standing there all along, watching the chasm that was now so wide open between him and Avni.

21

"You didn't need to be so cold to him," Sia said in a cool, non-judgemental voice as soon as Avni finished the call. "After all, he is taking care of Vivan in your absence.

Sia met Avni's eyes, "Just because of him, Mum and Dad are able to deal with this."

Avni knew that Sia was right. In fact, it was because of him that she was feeling a little reassured. Avni had started howling when she first heard her father's voice over the phone, informing about Vivan's condition. She had panicked so much. But after knowing that Mrs Joseph had called Aakash, she had settled a bit.

"Aakash is a thoroughly professional person," she said in a low voice, "He is too dedicated to his patients. Remember how he treated me when I had just joined. On my first emergency duty, when that young patient had died."

"But Vivan is not his patient." Sia looked at her again, half wondering what had happened to her sister. She was so ungrateful to him. Whatever must have happened between them, but after all, he was doing them a favour right now. She felt like telling Avni, but she avoided. Not the right time, she thought.

"He will do this for anyone in this world." Avni looked away, avoiding any eye contact with Sia. She didn't say that she still loved him and couldn't bear to talk to him again. If not for Vivan, she wouldn't have ever spoken to him again. It bought back all the memories and pain.

Sia was not very convinced by her reply. She knew Avni still loved him.

Vivan's X-Ray report was available soon. To Aakash's shock, the X-Ray report showed signs of peritonitis. He now knew that Vivan needed to be operated as quickly as possible, but he preferred to play it down in front of his grandparents. He didn't want them to panic. Although for the first time in his life as a doctor, he felt a sense of trepidation himself. "It should be okay," he told Mr and Mrs Trivedi. "Let's talk to the paediatrician."

"Vivan has to undergo surgery," Dr Ajay said. "But there should not be any problem. Prof Chandra is an excellent paediatric surgeon."

Aakash took a deep breath. The first thought that instantly hit him was that Avni was not around for such a critical decision. But he didn't want to alarm Mr and Mrs Trivedi. "Hmm…" He tried to appear calm, "It should be okay, but I guess…" He paused. "I know, Prof Chandra is a good surgeon, but it would be better if Dr Ramesh Mehta operates on him."

"You mean your father?" Dr Ajay looked startled with his suggestion. Being a batch-mate, he had a fair idea of the strained father-son relationship. But he preferred to take the professional approach, "He is a private practitioner. And Vivan is being treated here at this hospital. He should be operated here."

Mr Trivedi's eyes were jumping alternatively from one to another. As it was, he was finding it difficult to comprehend the series of events that were so swiftly unfolding in front of him. Mrs Trivedi couldn't control her tears. It was difficult for her to fathom that his beautiful grandson was going under the knife.

"Yes, I mean my father. He is the best paediatric surgeon in town." He looked straight into his eyes. Dr Ajay had a glimpse of the Aakash he knew from the long-time back, almost from the time of their graduation together. His firm and cold demeanour left no room for argument; anyway there was not an iota of doubt in the fact that Dr Ramesh Mehta was indeed the best paediatric surgeon.

"Well, let's ask Prof Chandra," Dr Ajay said and started dialling his number.

It was then when Avni called on her father's phone. She wanted to know about Vivan's X-Ray report, unaware that things had gone beyond that, surgery was being planned on her son. Mr Trivedi promptly handed over the phone to Aakash. Aakash could feel a shiver down his spine. He was now talking to Avni, mother of Vivan, the person who was to make the final decision about her son's condition. He had to convince her. Not an easy task, he thought, but he had to do it for Vivan's sake. Vivan was more of a patient than Avni's son today, and he must do best for him.

"My father tells me that Vivan needs an operation," Avni's voice was shaking.

"Yes, that's correct," he said in the familiar professional tone. Although today it wasn't original. He had to fake it. "Vivan has signs of impending peritonitis, and it is best not to go ahead with conservative treatment."

"And why do you want him to be operated by Dr Mehta?" Her anxiety-ridden words came too quickly.

"Because he is the best!" he said with a conviction that Avni found difficult to question. She instinctively knew that it was not for her. It was for Vivan that he was concerned. Still, she said, "I want to talk to Dr Chandra and seek his opinion."

"Of course!" Aakash said, "You must."

"I have no problem in operating on Vivan, but I guess Dr Mehta is better than me." Dr Chandra seemed to be in agreement with Aakash on this, much to Avni's chagrin. "Moreover, the surgical set up at Mehta's nursing home is excellent, better than our public hospital set up."

After the call, Avni silently bowed to that one person whom she could never stop loving and still could never go back to. Not knowing that one person had today finally lost all the hopes of having her back in his life, but had not given up on the promise of filling her life with happiness by taking care of her most precious possession, Vivan.

"How I wish to fly and be there with my baby." Avni's eyes were moist when she got off the phone. "Getting stuck up at a foreign land, so far from your child when he needs you most is insane."

Sia came closer to Avni and hugged her. "Don't worry, I am on the job," she said as she patted on her back, "We should be able to get the ticket on the first available flight that leaves London."

Sia then made her sister sit on the sofa and gave her a glass of water. When Avni looked a little settled, she asked about Vivan's operation.

"You know Aakash, the kind of man that he is, he would go to any extent to get Vivan the best treatment." Her eyes met Sia's, "He has arranged Vivan to be operated by his father."

"But he doesn't talk to his father, I guess," Sia said. "I remember you telling me about it."

"Perhaps he does, now." Avni sighed.

"I had never asked you about your relationship with Aakash." Her eyes held Avni's. "Do you love him?"

"But he doesn't," Avni absentmindedly said and immediately regretted it the next moment.

"Then why would he go out of his way to help Vivan?" Sia was baffled. "What made you think that he doesn't love you?"

"I can't tell you. I won't be able to stop my tears if I start telling you." Avni took a deep breath and looked away.

Sia was puzzled. Her sister never failed to surprise her. Today was no different. Avni had not said anything and had still managed to convey a lot.

Dr Mehta couldn't believe when his secretary informed that it was his son, Aakash who was on the phone on the other side. He promptly picked up the phone.

"Yes, my son," he said, "What can I do for you?" It was so long. His heart ached to hear his voice.

"Dad, we have a child with a history of intussusception," Aakash said without any preliminaries. "He has signs of peritonitis in X-Ray. And you have to operate him."

After ages, his son had asked him for something... anything. Who was he to refuse? He would have given anything to fulfill his wishes.

"Of course I will," he said without any asking any extra questions. "Get him transferred here."

"Thanks, Dad!" Aakash sounded very happy, "You are the best person to do the job."

For Dr Mehta, it was perhaps the best day in his life to have been honoured by his son, whom he had lost because of his own mistakes.

❖

Vivan was operated by Dr Mehta early in the morning. It was around 8 a.m. when he finished the surgery. Aakash was present in the theatre all along. Mr and Mrs Trivedi were anxiously waiting outside the operation theatre. They were thrilled to know that the surgery was successful and that Vivan was doing well. Mr Trivedi profusely thanked Dr Mehta and Aakash, while Mrs Trivedi kept wiping away her tears of relief and happiness. "We will keep Vivan under observation for some time," Dr Mehta informed them as he left for home.

Aakash stayed for a while. He left after ensuring proper arrangements for Avni's parents to stay at one of the private suites at his father's nursing home.

"Why couldn't Avni find someone like Aakash?" Mrs Trivedi commented when they were alone in their room. "How I always wanted her to marry someone as loving and caring as him."

Sia jumped with excitement, "You know, a few flights have resumed. And I just got confirmation from the airline that our seats have been confirmed."

Avni hugged Sia. "It's all because of you." She said, "You never gave up."

"For Vivan, I can do anything," Sia said. "Our flight is in the evening. We will reach Delhi by 3 a.m. tomorrow."

"And from there, we will be going straight to Dr Mehta's nursing home," Avni said, "I have to see Vivan the first thing after reaching there."

"Of course! Let's start packing our bags," Sia said. "I have already told Mum and Dad about it."

Avni's eyes turned moist. It was such a huge relief. She would be finally able to be with her Vivan. A big mountain of pain suddenly started lifting from her heart.

The next morning, after Vivan's surgery, for the first time in so many years, Mrs Mehta was in for a big surprise, definitely a pleasant one, though. Aakash was going with his father to the nursing home to see Vivan. Her heart filled with warmth when she saw them leaving home together, lost in deep conversation about Vivan's surgery and post-op progress. She silently thanked the child for bringing them together. She wondered about Aakash and Avni. Perhaps Vivan would also bring them together, she thought as she smiled to herself.

22

Avni and Sia had already cleared the immigration and security check at the airport, impatiently waiting for the flight to be announced, when suddenly Avni spotted someone, whom she would have given anything to evade. She was shocked to find her there. Not that she had anything against her, but the mere sight of her brought back all the memories of the pain, the regret, and the loss that she would have never wanted to visit ever again. Avni didn't wish Sia to know what she was feeling from inside. She merely lowered her gaze to avoid it. But the next moment, she was there.

"Avni!" Priya called her name. Avni almost froze. "*Why the hell she is here? What does she want from me?*"

Avni looked up. Sia also looked in her direction, at this new person whom she had never met in life. A lovely girl casually dressed in jeans and a sweater was standing in front of them.

"Hi!" Avni's cold response was neither missed by Priya, nor by Sia.

"Great to see you here," Priya was unperturbed. "So where you are heading to?"

"Delhi," Avni again tried to be formal, "Back home after attending a conference."

"I am going to Los Angeles," she said with a smile, "For some fun."

"Let's have coffee, guys," Priya spoke again as Sia was awestruck, listening to their conversation. "I guess we still have time for boarding."

In spite of her wanting to, Avni couldn't say no.

They had ordered for coffee and were waiting when suddenly Priya spoke, "You may not believe me, but I have wanted to meet you for the longest time. I am so glad I finally could." The surprised look on Avni's face didn't go unnoticed by both Priya and Sia. However, she continued, unperturbed,

"What I am going to tell you now is the only truth that ever existed," she said with a quivering voice, "Aakash loves you. He can never love anyone else. You are his past, present and future. You must have misunderstood him, but it's just you or no one else in his life. You taught him to laugh. You make him alive. His exists because of you. And he exists for you. Don't waste any more time. You are a very fortunate woman. Not everyone finds someone who loves them so much." And then she stopped, as abruptly as she had started. She couldn't continue anymore. She took a deep breath and looked at Avni. "I am lucky that today I could get a chance to convey all this to you. Literally, a godsent opportunity." She then smiled and held Avni's hand. Avni eyes met hers, and she smiled back.

Sia was stunned. So this was what her sister had never told her.

Avni couldn't believe her ears. Yes, she was listening to this from her, from Priya. It couldn't be true. It was like the most beautiful revelation anyone could imagine. For a moment, she repented for the lost time, the time they could have been together.

But instantly, the thought of pure, unadulterated joy of seeing Aakash overpowered her. All those dreams that they had woven together would be a reality now. Avni found herself lost deep in thoughts when flight announcement on the public system broke her reverie. There was not much time left for them to stay there any longer. It was now time for Avni and Sia to board the flight. Priya waved them goodbye as they queued to board. Although she wanted to call Aakash, she realized she had deleted his number long time back.

Once the flight was mid-air, floating high above the clouds Avni's mind drifted to the beautiful time that she had once shared with Aakash. How he had made her forget her painful past. How he loved Vivan. How quickly he had filled the void that had existed in their life. And in spite of all that, how she had misunderstood him. Tears suddenly welled up in her eyes. *Why did she let this happen? Why couldn't she be more reasonable? Why was she punishing Aakash for the things that Samir did to her? Why couldn't she let go of her fears and insecurities? Why didn't she even bother to clear things up with Aakash rather than leaving him in a hurry?*

Surprisingly, she realized she couldn't have done any better, for her past conditioning wouldn't have allowed her to do things differently. Perhaps she was paying the price of her original sin. She knew she couldn't undo the past, but she could still change the present and dream for the future. She promised herself to love him more than he could ever imagine. She would compensate for the lost time. She was getting a second chance, both with Vivan and Aakash, which was a gift that she would cherish forever. She didn't realize when she slept thinking about them, her most treasured possessions. Avni again saw them in her dream – All three of them walking together along the seashore, walking hand in hand and laughing together with their shadows growing with the rising sun. She was looking at those shadows when suddenly they started fading one by one and finally there was just a void left. She woke up with a vague feeling – like a fleeting thought that she couldn't catch. She looked around. Sia was sitting next to her, smiling at her. The flight was still above the clouds.

"Good morning!" Sia said, "We are going to land soon."

Avni instantly forgot all about the dream and smiled back at Sia. Avni could feel her heart racing with a joy unknown to her until now. "I can't believe I would be seeing Vivan." she said with excitement.

"And also Aakash." Sia spontaneously took her hand in her own, "I am so happy for you."

"But he doesn't know that you know the truth now, that you are ready to have him back in your life, does he?" Sia then suddenly looked at her with little scepticism in her voice. "What if he has found someone else?" She paused, "Sorry, I don't want to disappoint you, but just a thought."

"No, you are absolutely right, but out of sheer curiosity, I had browsed through my email spam folder once we had boarded the flight. That was the folder I had assigned his emails to after I had stopped seeing him."

"And you found something?" Sia was also curious now.

"Yes," Avni said, her eyes looking at a distance through the plane's window. "Here it is, written only a week before we left for London." She handed her phone to Sia.

Sia started reading.

Can't you just see me one more time? If we cannot be together again, then at least give me some false hope. Let me feel the pain, but at least I will live once more before I die. And perhaps would bring closure for me.

She looked at Avni. She was still looking outside. Tears were trickling down her cheeks. Sia wrapped her arm around Avni's shoulder.

"You are so fortunate to find him….again."

Avni smiled through her tears.

Soon there was the announcement. The flight was preparing to land. "What a wonderful homecoming!" Sia shouted.

23

Vivan was doing well after the surgery. He was started on liquids and was showing good progress. In fact, he had smiled at Aakash when he had gone to see him in the morning. Dr Mehta had advised Vivan to remain in the hospital for few more days. He didn't want to take any chance with Vivan. Vivan's grandparents had gladly accepted his advice.

Aakash had taken a day off from work. He hadn't been able to sleep the previous night, so anxious he was because of Vivan's operation. After checking on Vivan in the morning, he had decided to stay at home in the afternoon to catch up on his sleep. But as much as he would have wanted, sleep deserted him. Avni was on her way to Delhi. Mrs Trivedi had told him that she would be reaching Delhi early in the morning. And then she would be directly coming to the clinic from the airport. She wanted to see Vivan as soon as she reached here. Avni's parents believed it naturally that upon her arrival, Aakash would also be there. After all, for them, he was a close friend who had helped them with Vivan's treatment.

"We are so grateful for all your help. She would love to see you and thank you in person," Mrs Trivedi had said in the morning, "I am sure, you'd be there when she comes."

"Of course!" Mr Trivedi joined his wife, "It would probably be time for Dr Mehta's round and Aakash would be here anyway."

It was a dilemma that Aakash was not able to shake off from his head. He wanted to avoid Avni. But he couldn't say no. How could he? For them, he was a good friend of their daughter, a friend who had helped them in her absence and not her painful past that their daughter had rightly shed long before they could get to know him. Now Aakash didn't want to make her feel obliged. He didn't want her to feel that she owed him anything just because he had taken care of Vivan.

She had decided to leave him then. And he had respected her decision, even if it meant for him to stop existing. He knew that it must have taken enormous courage for Avni to love someone again. And that it must have been unimaginable for her to be deceived again. But he also knew that it was a great mistake for a man like him to fall in love, for he could never fall out of it.

Aakash was still feeling lost when his mind capriciously decided to be someone who he wasn't. He hated pretension all his life, but today he settled to be an actor, a fine one at that, for Avni's sake. He would just be a perfect friend to Avni who did his duty, something that was needed to be done. She must not feel uncomfortable in the presence of everyone. He would ensure that. Not knowing that Avni was thinking to do just the opposite.

Their plane landed at the airport at around five in the morning. After trying to clear immigration and customs as quickly as possible, Avni and Sia took a prepaid taxi and headed towards Mehta Hospital. Sia was watching how desperate her sister looked. Avni was repeatedly checking the time and almost pleading with the taxi driver to drive as fast as possible. Sia had to interrupt her at times and tell the driver to not to go above the speed limit. In almost less than two hours after landing, they were at the gates of the hospital. Avni got out of the car and sprinted towards the reception, waving at Sia to take care of luggage.

Avni's heart lifted at the sight of Vivan. She took him in her arms and hugged him. Vivan squealed with delight and hugged her back. There were no traces of trauma. The older Trivedis were overjoyed to be able to safely return to their daughter, her most treasured possession. For a few moments, no one said anything. It seemed all of them just wanted to drench in the relief and happiness of forgetting the nightmare of the last few days. It was Sia who broke the silence by showing Vivan the new toy, the racing car, his most favourite thing that she had bought from London. He wanted to play and tried wriggling out of Avni's embrace, but couldn't.

"He has gone too weak," Mr Trivedi said. "It will take some time for him to fully recover."

Avni then put him down on the bed. He wanted to play with the toy. Sia got busy with him. She then looked towards her parents. Suddenly, in a matter of a week, they seemed much older. The wrinkles had deepened. She hugged her mother and then her father. Sia looked at them. How long it had been that Avni had embraced him.

"Mum.... Dad!" Avni looked at them with tears in her eyes, "I can never thank you enough for all that you have done for me in life." She took a deep breath, "But today, you have given my Vivan back to me! I don't know how to even thank you."

"Vivan is also our baby," Mr Trivedi said as he fondly looked at Avni. "It was our duty to look after him." He then paused and looked at his wife who was caressing their daughter, "But you should thank Dr Aakash." He then paused for a moment as if thinking about something, "I have never seen such a dedicated person. It's because of him that we could save Vivan." For the first time in her life, Avni saw his eyes getting moist. "I never showed to your Mum, I didn't want to frighten her. But I was petrified."

Sia, his ideal child, couldn't see her father feeling so overwhelmed. She instantly got up and hugged her father. "It's alright, Dad! Our nightmare has ended. Now it's all good."

24

Aakash was driving his car with his father sitting next to him. The driver had called early in the morning today to inform Dr Mehta that he won't be able to come for work. Aakash offered him a lift. He would have gone there anyway to have a look at Vivan before proceeding off to his work at Delhi Medical College and Hospital. It was raining outside. He turned on the wipers. His eyes went to the windscreen in front of him. It appeared just like the never-ending cycles of his mind – cloudy-clear-cloudy-clear. He silently hoped that Avni was not there. Either her plane was delayed, or she had left by the time he reached there. At one moment, everything seemed so confusing, but the next moment, it appeared that it would all be okay. As he had imagined, he could just pretend to be her friend, and it would all be natural.

"Be careful!" his father blurted as a truck being driven in the next lane came too close to their car, "It's raining. You have to be very alert."

He wondered if he could ever tell his father what was bothering him, now that both were having better terms after Vivan's surgery. "I will be, Dad!" He simply responded. Soon they reached Mehta Hospital. Parking was across the road from the hospital. They started walking towards the hospital, waiting for the pedestrian signal to light up.

"Do you want me to start the round from Vivan's room?" Dr Mehta said, "I guess you would then be free to go to your work."

"Thanks, Dad!" he said, "That would be good."

Dr Mehta and Aakash were in front of the room allotted to Vivan. Dr Mehta knocked at the door before stepping in for the rounds. Instantly, a face that he hadn't seen before appeared behind the door.

"Dr Mehta," he introduced himself.

"Avni. Vivan's mother," she replied as she bowed to him.

"Great!" He smiled, "Welcome back, Dr Avni! Your son is a brave child."

"Thank you, Dr Mehta," she said as her eyes looked over his shoulder. Aakash was standing there. Avni met his dark brown eyes. She held her eyes for a moment before he looked away. "It's all because of you that Vivan could be saved."

"Of course not!" Dr Mehta said smilingly, "You are a doctor. You know it. We just do our best. Rest is in god's hands." He then turned back to look at Aakash, "But it's your friend whom you should be thanking."

This was *the* moment Aakash wanted to evade. He wished to disappear from there. He never wanted to take credit for Vivan. For him, Avni was worth more than anything he could have ever done for her. She could never owe anything to him. Avni looked in Aakash's direction. "You are absolutely right Dr Mehta!" With a fondness in her voice, she said. "I owe him a lot." She didn't say that she owed her second chance at life to him. That she had made an enormous mistake in understanding him. That she would do anything in her power to undo the mistake and start again from where they had left, but only if he was willing to forgive her.

Avni looked at Aakash expectedly after not getting any immediate response from him. "It's okay!" he said with a smile. A smile that was as deceptive as was his face, completely unreadable. "I haven't done anything great. I would have done this for anyone. But Vivan is certainly special for me."

For Avni, those words were like first rain falling on parched earth. She wanted to hug him and tell him that he was also as special to them and they were going to be together forever. But she would tell him this very soon, she thought.

Mr and Mrs Trivedi were spellbound, looking at Aakash with awe mixed with praise. How fortunate they would have been if Avni had married someone like him. How happy their daughter would have been! While on the other hand, Sia was only waiting for the surreal moment when Avni was going to confess her feelings to Aakash.

"He is doing very well!" Dr Mehta looked around and announced. "He can be discharged today. I will order for it." He then looked at Avni, "You can make arrangements to take him home by lunch time."

Avni thanked Dr Mehta once again. Her parents also joined her.

Dr Mehta then turned to leave when he looked at Aakash. "Do you want to stay more or would want to leave for work?"

Avni's eyes travelled to him. Her eyes held Aakash's. It was like they wanted to capture his image so that it could never be taken away from them. She wished that he said 'Yes.' But he said 'No' as he slowly removed his gaze, "I have to leave now."

And both of them left, almost as abruptly as they had arrived.

25

Avni was still contemplating about contacting Aakash, ready to surprise him, confessing her love once again, albeit after going through the trial by fire of pain when she got a call from Mrs Malhotra from the SMILE foundation for HIV orphan children. The foundation was holding a charity event to honour young children who had just graduated from the primary school.

"Imagine, Dr Avni," Mrs Malhotra said, "We were not sure even about their survival after such a terrible tragedy, of losing both their parents when they were barely out of their cribs, and today they have successfully completed their primary school."

"Wonderful news, Mrs Malhotra"! Avni chirped, "This indeed deserves celebration. We should cheer for their achievement."

"But our celebration won't be possible without you and Dr Aakash, two people who so dedicatedly made this journey possible." Mrs Malhotra's voice genuinely echoed her sentiments. "We would be obliged if you can join us on the forthcoming Saturday evening. In fact, I called you after not getting any response to our postal invitation."

"Sorry about that, but I was out of the country," Avni said while her mind was wondering how Aakash had responded, but she didn't say anything. "I just returned yesterday. I would join the work from next week."

"I guess Dr Aakash was also away," Mrs Malhotra said, "We didn't hear back from him also."

Avni was speechless for a moment, not knowing why he hadn't responded to the invitation, unaware that he wanted to be away from anything that reminded him about her. Then she said, "He might have been busy."

"Probably," Mrs Malhotra said. "I will try calling him again."

Aakash had just finished his OPD when he got a call from Mrs Malhotra. Briefly, he thought of not answering the call and let go of the whole thing, but some unseen power forced him to respond. Mrs Malhotra was about to give up when she heard Aakash on the other side. She repeated the request she had just made to Avni, very hopeful of his affirmative response. Instead, Aakash's lukewarm response came out as a little surprise to her. She remembered how last time he had not only excitedly participated in the function with Avni, but had promised to be a permanent attendee of these charity events for the orphans. Mrs Malhotra could not have ever realized that if Avni was the reason for him to attend the function the last year, Avni was the reason for him to avoid participating now. However much he tried, Aakash couldn't bring himself to ask if Avni was visiting, a question that would have made his decision quick and precise. He would have excused himself and apologized to Mrs Malhotra and would have never come to the function if he could know Avni's decision to attend. Aakash was clear that everything, whatever it was, was all over between them and he wouldn't want to make her uncomfortable by appearing alongside her without her wanting to. Only if he had known how much Avni was dying to see her.

"I will certainly try to come, if I can." Aakash half-heartedly tried to reassure Mrs Malhotra, "Hopefully I don't have any emergency to attend." Then there was the silence that hung hard in the air, with so many words unspoken.

She didn't insist any further and accepted his words of reassurance with much grace.

Somehow after getting the invitation from Mrs Malhotra, Avni happily decided to wait for the event to meet Aakash rather than trying to call him on the phone. She was not sure if she could talk to him on the phone, the deluge of adoration and longing amidst the fog of misunderstandings would smudge the pure love that was going to be shared once again. Avni had no qualms about asking for his forgiveness; in her world, to accept one's mistake unconditionally, infinitely empowered the love to withstand any storm. She was sure that Aakash would not be able to hold anything against her when she would meet him. He would forgive her instantly as he was the only one who could understand why she did what she did; why she didn't even have the option to ask for his explanation for she had already exhausted all her options with Samir and was not left with any reserve.

Keeping her hope intact, her faith strong and her love invincible, she anxiously waited for Saturday evening.

Aakash was not so fortunate. He didn't have anything to look forward to. He had already lost Avni, he didn't want to lose her beautiful memories by being at a place where she wouldn't want to see him. He wondered if he could ever separate from those beautiful memories if he safely keeps locked them in his heart away from the world. He wouldn't want her to endure any more pain because of him. His only happiness was to see her happy with Vivan, and for that, he had to be away from her life. In fact, he had decided to finish his professional commitments as quickly as possible and quietly disappear from the hospital and the city, or perhaps the country for good, to never cause any inconvenience to Avni ever again. Several times in the day, he wanted to call Mrs Malhotra and confirm his inability to attend, but every time, something stopped him.

On the day of the event

Avni's anxious wait to see Aakash was almost over. After spending the whole day selecting the best outfit for the event, she decided to wear the same saree she had worn for the event last time. It reminded her so many beautiful things. There were so many fond memories the cherry red saree must have witnessed on that day; his tenderness, his happiness on seeing her happy with children, his interest in her life for the first time. She wondered if Aakash would be surprised by her choice, if he would also acknowledge her choice with the same intensity as she was feeling.

Once inside her car, she could not stop herself from daydreaming. How could she not? Not everyone is as fortunate as her; she had undoubtedly traversed a road that had a lot of twists and turns, peaks and ditches, but ultimately, she was going to reach her destination.

This time we will be together forever, not going to be separated by any storm of life. I know I have not been the best version of myself, but I promise, I will try to be one this time.

There was still time. The event was starting at 7 p.m., but she drove to the venue as fast as she could.

On the day of the event, as soon as Aakash got up in the morning, he made up his mind about the evening. After spending almost the entire night agonizing over his options, he decided that it was best to not to attend the SMILE function. He would call Mrs Malhotra to personally express his inability to come, he thought to himself. How desperately he wanted to talk to Avni when she had misunderstood him about Priya; confident of clearing all the misunderstanding in one stroke if she had agreed to see him, but now things had gone too far. Avni had perhaps reconciled; she was looking cheerful after her Europe tour, he thought. Maybe she had moved on when he was still grieving his loss. Now it was best to leave her alone. *Sometimes it's best to leave things halfway if it can't be taken to a conclusion. However self-defeating and painful it might sound, but at least it stops you from investing in something which has no future.*

Although he had made up his mind, he had no idea why a feeble flame inside his heart was refusing to accept his decision. It was hopelessly hopeful of some miracle. With his foggy thoughts, he joined her mother for breakfast. Mrs Mehta instantly noticed something terribly wrong with her son. Not that he was happy during the last few months, but today it was entirely different. He seemed so out of sync. On much prodding, Aakash unwittingly told everything to her, but as briefly as possible.

Mrs Mehta silently listened to every bit his son told her, but she suggested that he should follow his heart rather than his mind, for the heart could only decipher signals from the immortal soul that journeys from life to life. The mind didn't have that power.

"Perhaps your souls know each other from different lifetimes," she said reflectively. "That's why in spite of so many contradictions, you two have met in this life."

Sometimes you just want to hear what you really want to do. Coming from someone you trust doesn't give it a stamp of approval, but only resonates with your hidden resolve to manifest it. Perhaps it was the same for Aakash. He just wanted to hear from his mother what he would have done anyway.

Armed with an unknown hope that had no logic, no meaning or no signs of fulfillment in sight, Aakash left for the evening function. It was raining, her mother asked him to be careful when she waved him goodbye. On the way, he tried different songs, but somehow he couldn't concentrate. His mind was on a roller-coaster ride, unable to keep it away from Avni. He recollected every small detail from the first time they had met, to the last day they were together. He heard a few honks here and there from the side lanes and behind and tried to correct himself, but then again, he would get lost in his thoughts.

Avni, I talked to you. I embraced you. I laughed with you. I cried for you. You can run away from me, but you can't take away the memories we built together. You can be angry with me, you may not forgive me, but I will wait for you till eternity.

Aakash then, all of a sudden, heard a loud honking sound. It was raining hard. He looked at his rear-view mirror; he couldn't see anything.

26

The programme had started right on time. Avni had reached ten minutes earlier. She was received by Mrs Malhotra and was served coffee before the program. Once the clock struck 7, Avni along with Mrs Malhotra and other dignitaries were requested to take their seat in the front row. Avni sat next to the chair that had Aakash's name on it. Her heart was jumping with excitement and joy of seeing Aakash again. Although the programme had started promptly, her eyes were scanning the entrance gate in anticipation of his arrival. For a moment, she found herself irritated with him for being late in spite of being such a punctual person, but slowly she realized that for now, she didn't have that power over him; she had to earn that power once again. She smiled to herself with the thought. *Yes, this is what her resolve for today was.*

The second item was a dance sequence that was put together by Shiv, one of her favourite child from the orphanage. Aakash had still not arrived, but for a few minutes, she couldn't take her eyes off the stage, such was the performance by the young children. She realized her phone had been vibrating in her handbag. She discreetly pulled out the phone to hurriedly check the message, half expecting it to be from Aakash. The name Dr Neha flashed on the screen. Avni was definitely a little indulgent in her thoughts. Still, she felt disappointed at not receiving any message from him. She wondered what message Dr Neha had for her on a weekend night, but she knew she could not ignore her. She opened the message.

Aakash had an accident. He is in ICU. Please come soon to the hospital.

She couldn't believe it; she read it again. She then hurriedly excused herself after taking permission from Mrs Malhotra and walked outside into the hallway. Once outside the hall, she reread it. Then again, but everything remained the same, no word moved from its place to alter its meaning or to accommodate any change. She was now staring at one of the scariest truths of her life. In spite of her best efforts, she could not gather the courage to call Dr Neha to find out the extent of the injury. Then suddenly Avni felt that she could not stand anymore. A watchman was watching her; he came rushing to help her, but she fainted. A small crowd had assembled around her when she opened her eyes again in a few minutes. She then insisted on going to the hospital immediately, even though Mrs Malhotra and others asked her to rest.

Avni rushed back to ICU to see Aakash, the same place that she had chosen to be posted to stay away from him. The irony of it wasn't lost on her as she neared the hospital complex. She got a little perturbed by the crowd of doctors outside the ICU. Everyone, senior doctors, registrars, senior and junior, were standing there. She could see Aakash's parents in the crowd; her fears worsening with every passing minute. She was still trying to comprehend everything when Dr Neha touched her shoulder from behind.

It was difficult for her to face Avni, but then she said slowly, "It was a massive accident. His car was hit by a tractor-trolley." Avni looked at her in disbelief. No words could come out of her mouth; she felt her mouth getting dry. "He has suffered critical injuries." Dr Neha didn't elaborate any further though she knew that what she was saying was an understatement; Aakash was much worse. Dr Kapoor had already indicated to her that there was a very slim chance of his survival. Avni instantly decided to see him. Dr Neha nodded her head in silence. Avni was anyway posted there, albeit on leave. A new intern who failed to recognize Avni stopped her as she made way to the changing room to change into ICU gear. "I am a junior fellow, posted here. I was on leave." She almost whispered and quickly disappeared inside. Mrs Mehta was watching Avni ever since she had arrived. She felt a sudden hope in the form of Avni; perhaps his love would save him, if nothing else. Her eyes followed Avni until the moment she went inside.

Once inside, for a moment Avni stood unmoved at a little distance from Aakash's bed, watching with anxious eyes, the scene that had unfolded in front of her like a nightmare. He was connected to all sorts of tubes and monitors. But then, unaware of her surrounding, of the army of doctors around Aakash, she moved closer to his bed. She looked at his face. His eyes were closed, but his face looked as handsome as ever. It seemed as if he was sleeping and would get up to claim his rightful position in her life. Suddenly, a moment later, he opened his eyes; it was as if he had just been waiting for her. Aakash met her warm brown eyes. She held his eyes for a moment before he closed it again. And this time, it was forever. Dr Kapoor shortly declared him dead.

Avni stood there motionless, having no idea of her surroundings or what was going on. She stoically looked at the man who loved her, who made her believe in love again, a man who had been true to his words till the last moment, if only she had believed him… if only she had not let her past cloud her present. She then slowly leaned toward his lifeless body, kissed him on the forehead and buried her head in his chest as if to listen to the heartbeat that no machine could ever hear.

Epilogue

It was early in the morning, a day after Aakash's funeral. Avni was sitting with Sia in the backyard.

"Before I stopped seeing him," Avni said, "we were sitting here on that day, Aakash looked at me and said, 'Can you see there?' He pointed at a distance, 'There, beyond the horizon?' I just looked there and then looked back at him. He then said, 'Remember you said once that the sky and earth just appear to meet at the horizon but they never actually meet.' He then took my hand in his own, kissed it and said, 'But I will be meeting you even beyond that.'

"And I didn't question it. Aakash is like that sky, forever with me, in every step. We will meet again on the horizon, and this time, it will be for eternity. And though we might not be destined to be together in this life, my soul will always be one with him, forever. I can never feel the way I have felt for him for anyone else. He will always remain a special part of me. 'Love' might not be the right word. He lives in my every breath, every heartbeat."

Sia didn't say anything. But she thought to herself as she caught a glimpse of Avni's forlorn eyes. They might be separated by the chasm of life and death in the current moment, but one day, these two will be united, never to leave each other's side again.